Look what people are saying about Heather MacAllister

"Witty, romantic, sexy and fun…and
Heather's books aren't bad either."
—*New York Times* bestselling author Christina Dodd

"Curling up with a Heather MacAllister romance
is one of my favorite indulgences."
—#1 *New York Times* bestselling author
Debbie Macomber

"Funny, fabulous, fantastic! Heather MacAllister
is at the top of my must-read list."
—RITA® Award winner and *USA TODAY*
bestselling author Barbara Dawson Smith

"Smart, witty and fun…no one does it better
than Heather MacAllister."
—Award-winning author Amanda Stevens

"A one-sitting read for me. I got so caught up
in this story that I really didn't want it to end."
—*The Best Reviews* on *Male Call*

"The plot was inspired, the dialogue was witty and
the secondary characters were extraordinary."
—*Writers Unlimited* on
How to Be the Perfect Girlfriend

Blaze™

Dear Reader,

In September 2008, Hurricane Ike hit the Houston-Galveston area and I missed the whole thing. I was at a writing retreat in the Pacific Northwest and all I could do was watch the news reports as the storm headed for my family and friends. Everybody is fine and we had minimal damage, but I didn't know for several days because there was no electricity, no phone, no cell service and no Internet. Oh, and no flights into the airport. I stood in line at SeaTac with thousands of other displaced passengers and discovered that it would be five days before I could get on a flight.

Christina Dodd and her husband, Scott, graciously took me into their home. So while my family was sweltering and cleaning up hurricane debris, I was suffering in perfect fall weather, sampling lovely wines, shopping and trying to feel guilty. *His Little Black Book* takes place during a tropical storm that will give you just a hint of what happens during a hurricane. Or so they tell me.

Best wishes,

Heather MacAllister

Heather MacAllister

HIS LITTLE BLACK BOOK

TORONTO • NEW YORK • LONDON
AMSTERDAM • PARIS • SYDNEY • HAMBURG
STOCKHOLM • ATHENS • TOKYO • MILAN • MADRID
PRAGUE • WARSAW • BUDAPEST • AUCKLAND

Recycling programs
for this product may
not exist in your area.

ISBN-13: 978-0-373-79531-4

HIS LITTLE BLACK BOOK

This edition published by arrangement with Harlequin Books S.A.

For questions and comments about the quality of this book please contact us at *Customer_eCare@Harlequin.ca.*

www.eHarlequin.com

Printed in U.S.A.

ABOUT THE AUTHOR

Heather MacAllister lives near the Texas gulf coast where, in spite of the ten-month growing season and plenty of humidity, she can't grow plants. She's a former music teacher who married her high school sweetheart on the Fourth of July, so is it any surprise that their two sons turned out to be a couple of firecrackers? Heather has written more than forty romantic comedies, which have been translated into twenty-six languages and published in dozens of countries. She's won a Romance Writers of America Golden Heart Award, *RT Book Reviews* awards for best Harlequin Romance and best Harlequin Temptation, and is a three-time RITA® Award finalist. When she's not writing stories about where life has its quirks, Heather collects vintage costume jewelry, loves fireworks displays, computers that behave and sons who answer their mother's e-mails. You can visit her at www.HeatherMacAllister.com.

Books by Heather MacAllister

HARLEQUIN BLAZE

473—UNDRESSED

To Christina Dodd and her husband, Scott.
Thanks for sheltering this hurricane refugee.

Prologue

"JONATHAN?"

Emerging from his office, Jonathan Black did an about face and schooled his features to hide his impatience. He was on his way to discuss advertising strategy with a new client and it was Friday afternoon. Friday. Afternoon. The sooner the meeting was over, the sooner the weekend would begin.

"What's up, Cammy?"

Cammy Phillips, his very unassuming, but very devoted, assistant smiled eagerly. "You know how you said to let you know anytime the beach house is vacant?"

"Yeah."

"It's about to be vacant. Adrian Dean is leaving early because of the storm warnings."

"No kidding? What a wuss. Who else knows?"

"Just you."

"Yes!" Jonathan pumped his fist into the air.

"And," Cammy continued a little breathlessly, "I went ahead and reserved it for you."

"You are a goddess among women!" He blew her a kiss.

She actually blushed.

Grinning, Jonathan wheeled around and headed to the

conference room. This was great. Peck and Davilla Media Management owned a sweet beach house in Surfside, Texas, a little over an hour's drive from the Houston office. Weekends when the house wasn't being used for company business were rare, highly prized and often used as currency to get favors from Production. With more advance warning, that's what Jonathan would do, but it was already three-thirty, so he'd just have to make the sacrifice and use the beach house himself. He deserved it after being scheduled for an initial client meeting on a Friday afternoon and he knew who had done the scheduling: Mia Weiss in the traffic department.

Mia, Mia, Mia. He shook his head.

He liked her and there was serious potential there, and the new short haircut actually looked sexy on her. Yeah. Short hair. Sure surprised him and he liked surprise. But. Yes, but. Mia had made it clear that she wanted more than good times. Jonathan didn't want long term. He had enough trouble with short term. To be honest, she'd only asked for exclusivity. Eminently reasonable.

But when it came to women, Jonathan wasn't reasonable. Didn't want to be. Didn't have to be.

So the late meeting was Mia's way of messing with the start of his weekend. Nicely played.

Asking her to the beach house would be a waste. Time to move on.He'd have Cammy send her the usual lovely parting gift: a spa basket with an afternoon pampering certificate for a facial and a "mani-pedi." A classy ending meant friendly exes. And since he had a lot of exes, life was much easier if they were friendly.

So, who was gonna be the lucky girl?

As he walked, Jonathan whipped out his iPhone and scrolled through his electronic little black book. He needed someone casual...spontaneous...hot. He needed Jennifer Allen, the bartender at Junipers.

Entering the conference room, he scanned the

occupants—creative teams hoping for a crack at a new account, a guy from Production, a few interns and Ross, the senior art director and Jonathan's preferred go-to guy. The client hadn't arrived yet.

Neither had Sophie What's-Her-Name, the ambitious junior copywriter who'd shown Ross up on Monday. She was talented, and she was cute, and she had focus. And a lot of nerve. Ross was going to have to watch her. Jonathan certainly was. He was mildly disappointed that she wasn't here now, but he wasn't surprised. Ross couldn't have his junior staff hijacking client meetings, no matter how much the client liked their ideas.

But in the meantime, the beach house awaited. Jonathan thumbed a text message as a couple of interns set up the PowerPoint and Ross answered his cell. "Jonathan, reception says Terry Simmons is on the way up."

Nodding to Ross, Jonathan spoke while he continued with the text he wanted to get out before the meeting began. "Could you go meet him at the elevator? Thanks."

He quickly finished the message. Up for a hurricane party? Scored company beach house for weekend! Might run late. Will meet you there. Pick up steaks and breakfast? Key code #3214.

He was in the process of highlighting "Allen, Jennifer" when out of the corner of his eye, he saw Ross and Simmons approaching and glanced up. First he noticed the funny look on Ross's face and then he saw the stunning brunette who preceded him into the conference room. Behind her, Ross mouthed, "Terry Simmons."

That was Terry Simmons? Terry Simmons was a woman? No, not just a woman. A Woman.

A womanly woman with impressive womanly parts that strained against the buttons of her blouse. Her hair was pulled back and she rocked the sexy square glasses she wore.

It was the naughty librarian of his fantasies. Of any man's fantasies.

She tugged on her suit jacket and Jonathan immediately yanked his gaze northward and kept it firmly fixed on her face as he stood to greet her.

"Ms. Simmons, I'm Jonathan Black, Creative Director." He smiled directly into her (alluring brown) eyes and grasped her (sensuously smooth) hand. He let an extra beat go by. Very important, that extra moment.

Rush the initial greeting and the client felt less valued and less inclined to approve campaigns. It was pretty much the same when approaching women, too.

"I'm here to learn all about you and what you want so Peck and Davilla can make it happen." He spoke with a practiced, warm sincerity accompanied by a practiced, warm smile. Maybe he kicked the smile up a notch.

As he released her hand, Terry Simmons blinked behind her smart-girl glasses.

He pulled out a chair at the conference table. "Would you like some coffee? A soft drink?"

"Just water, thanks." She smiled.

Was there a little added warmth in the smile? Why, yes, he believed there was.

Jonathan had a good feeling about this. As an intern poured water and everyone got settled, he returned to his seat and picked up his iPhone. If Jennifer couldn't make it, perhaps the luscious Terry Simmons might enjoy a weekend at the beach.

"Jonathan?"

At the sound of Terry's husky, seductive voice, he glanced up.

"I brought our current Flex-Time brochures to give everyone an idea about the company." She pushed a bundle across the table. "I'm open to any ideas." Her generous lips curved upward.

Open to any ideas. Message received. *It's good to be me.* Quickly tapping Send, Jonathan pocketed his cell and reached for the brochures.

Had he not been distracted, he might have noticed that in his electronic little black book, "Allen, Jennifer" was perilously close to "ALL"—close enough that it would have behooved him to double check which line he'd highlighted before sending the text.

But he didn't.

Text and the Single Girl

1

SOPHIE CALLAHAN SQUEALED and clamped her hand over her mouth. Her cell had just buzzed with an incoming text: Up for a hurricane party? Scored company beach house for weekend! Might run late. Will meet you there. Pick up steaks and breakfast? Key code #3214.

It was from Jonathan Black, Peck and Davilla's handsome, charismatic, talented, dynamic, sexy and irresistible Creative Director. Sigh and double sigh.

Sophie read the message three times, just to make sure she hadn't hallucinated it. Then she glanced around the room of copywriters, production artists, junior designers and image developers. In other words, newbies, all hoping to climb out of the pit. And it looked as though, she, Sophie Callahan, had just hauled herself over the edge.

No one else held a phone. Sophie waited, listening for buzzes and chirps. Had anyone else from the pit been invited to the party?

No? Then she'd really and truly caught the eye of Jonathan Black. And in a good way. Clutching her phone, she closed her eyes and exhaled, feeling relief more than anything. Relief that she'd accomplished a goal for which she'd sacrificed her entire social life.

For a year, she'd targeted Jonathan Black as the Creative Director she wanted to work with. For a year, she'd studied his past ad campaigns, analyzed his style, figured out which Peck and Davilla creatives he favored and studied *their* styles, and then put herself around them whenever she could. For a year, she'd volunteered for scut work and had done favors—many favors. She'd learned as much as she could and she'd given away ideas.

And the senior creatives had taken those ideas and used them as their own, especially Ross, one of the art directors.

That was okay. That was how the game was played. But Sophie knew when they used her ideas and they knew when they used her ideas. And after she disingenuously and publicly gushed her delight that they'd found her idea worthy, others knew it, too.

But it was her audacity during last Monday's meeting that must have finally pinged Jonathan's radar.

Ross's team had been pitching the second time to a retirement developer who'd hated their first ideas. All of them. Jonathan was sitting in as they'd scrambled not to lose the account. Knowing this, Sophie had intercepted an intern from Production and offered to deliver last-minute mock-ups to the meeting.

And then she'd stayed, ignoring pointed glances and a long look from Jonathan.

Sophie had studied this campaign as she'd studied the others and she didn't like it. It wasn't all that much different from the first one. Ross and his team weren't getting it, and Sophie could tell the clients didn't think so, either.

The P&D team was treating the retirement community as though it housed relics from an ancient civilization. The people in the illustrations didn't look like her grandparents. Her grandparents traveled, they volunteered—they went to the gym, for Pete's sake. They didn't spend their days sitting on a bench surrounded by azaleas and grinning goofily at each other like the couple in the picture Ross held.

And that's when Sophie had laughed. The room had grown tense and silent and the small sound drew everyone's attention. Not what she'd planned, but she brazened it out.

She gestured to the picture. "They're so not my grandparents. My grandparents are all about use it or lose it."

"And these two look like they've lost it," one of the client reps said, which was exactly what Sophie had been going to say.

Aware of Jonathan's sharp, unsmiling gaze upon her, she was glad she hadn't.

"This is—" one of the Worthington (Because You're Worth It) reps waved at the display and slumped in his seat "—depressing."

"The presentation reflects the tone you told us you were going for," Jonathan reminded them. "We stayed on message."

"We said 'upscale serenity,' not 'sit around and wait for the white light.'"

Jonathan interrupted the nervous chuckles. "So we don't want to emphasize calm and peaceful." He gestured for Ross to remove the storyboard. "Now we know. Don't feel you have to stick with your original idea. Let us kick this around and come at it from another direction."

The Worthington people exchanged looks and the rep spoke. "Jonathan, I don't think we're on the same wavelength."

Wave. Sophie's cue. "What about Ross's cruise idea?" Which was actually Sophie's idea. Which she'd just thought of.

"Cruise?" one of the clients asked.

Ross sent her a murderous glance and shook his head. "It was just a thought. It didn't fit the Worthington image."

But Jonathan had picked up on the client's interest. "They

want to go in a different direction. Maybe it fits now. Outline the idea for us."

Heart pounding, Sophie was afraid she'd gone too far. "My grandparents are always saying they could live on a cruise ship, so Ross was thinking about cruising through retirement and making the ads all bright and peppy like a cruise line's instead of lifeless and boring." Oops. She hadn't meant to say "lifeless and boring." Never criticize the client's idea. To his face. And never never never say anything negative about a pitch.

The Worthington people perked up. Ross, pro that he was, was already sketching out a few ideas. "When I saw the plans for your complex, I remember thinking that living there would be like being on a permanent vacation." And he was off.

Sophie stayed quiet, aware that Jonathan was studying her. She met his eyes once and smiled before turning her attention to Ross's extemporaneous presentation. Well, not *all* her attention. Jonathan wasn't the type of man a woman could ignore.

After the clients had left, just when Ross had been about to lay into her, Jonathan approached. "Great save, Ross." They exchanged a look. The other man gave a tight nod and retreated, but Sophie knew she'd hear about it later.

"What's your name?" Jonathan asked her.

"Sophie Callahan."

He pulled out his phone. "You've got balls, Sophie Callahan."

"I—"

"Don't ever do that again."

She clamped her mouth shut.

His gaze flicked over her. "I need your contact info."

Her voice sounding eager in spite of her best efforts, Sophie supplied it.

Jonathan entered her number and pocketed his phone. "You're lucky the cruise angle worked."

And did she say "thanks" and leave it at that? No. "It wasn't luck. I studied the account and I researched the demographics."

"Your grandparents," he said dryly.

"And their friends." She met his gaze. No use backing down now, even though her heart drummed so hard she could hear her pulse.

Something shifted in his eyes. He liked beautiful women, Sophie knew. Everyone knew. And he liked them with a certain sensual seasoning. Sophie was not beautifully seasoned. She was cute. And energetic. Not perky—energetic. There was a difference.

She wasn't Jonathan's type romantically, but a dinner out wouldn't be such a bad thing, since she could impress him during some one-on-one time. Sophie had no illusions about Jonathan. He was not a long-term guy, but he was enormously talented and she wanted the experience of working with him. If it took a couple of dates to get that chance, fine.

"We work in teams," he told her.

"So I've heard."

"You're not a team player."

"Maybe I need a better team."

Suddenly, he grinned. "Maybe you do."

A beat passed and Sophie stopped breathing. *Please, please, please put me on your team.*

His expression turned speculative. "You and Ross bounce off each other pretty good."

"Ross?" *No. No-no-no-no-no.* "He likes to work alone."

"I know. But creatively, he might need some shaking up. You strike me as the sort of person who shakes things up."

The man was toying with her. She could see it in his eyes. Talk about a disastrous pairing—for Sophie, anyway. Ross had used her ideas before and if she were officially assigned to his team, she knew she'd never get credit for anything. Never build her portfolio.

"Once concrete sets, it doesn't shake," she said. "It cracks and breaks."

"Careful, Sophie." Jonathan gave her a hard stare. "Ross has been around a long time. He's made a lot of contacts. And you need more than one good idea to build a career."

I've had lots of ideas. Several are in current ads. But she hadn't said anything. By that time, she'd said enough.

After he'd left, Sophie had dropped into a chair in the empty conference room and put her head between her knees. Ross? She was going to end up with Ross? It could have been worse. Jonathan could have fired her.

But now, just four days later, here was an invitation to one of his legendary beach parties! Maybe he wasn't going to assign her to Ross after all.

"You must have a *hot* date tonight."

Sophie opened her eyes to find Aire-An, her partner with the stupidly weird name, looking at her from across their desk. As though the affected spelling would make her stand out.

"It's got possibilities." Sophie didn't have a boyfriend. Not that she didn't want a boyfriend, but right now she didn't have time.

"New guy?"

"New opportunity." She set her phone down and closed her laptop. "I've got tons to do, so I'm taking off."

"Early?" Aire-An goggled at her. "You never leave early. I'm not sure you leave at all."

"That's what it takes to get ahead." She tried not to sound self-righteous, but honestly, as a partner, Aire-An had been an anchor. And not in a steadying way, but a holding back way.

"Yeah, well, I want to have a life, too."

Sophie cleared off her desk. "The way I see it is that we're always going to be working crazy hours, so I might as well be working crazy hours on a big project for more money."

"And more stress." Aire-An waggled her fingers at Sophie. "Go. Take off. Have a normal Friday night for once."

It had better not be normal, Sophie thought as she took the stairs to the lobby so she wouldn't attract notice by waiting for the elevator. See, it was the attention to little details that would get her ahead.

As she crossed the glass-enclosed walkway over the street to the parking garage, she noticed another detail, one maybe not so little. Clouds. And not fluffy, white, friendly clouds, but angry, gray clouds brushing past the downtown skyscrapers.

What had happened to the sun? How sad that she hadn't known the weather had changed. When Sophie got out of the pit and into a room with a window, she'd know what the weather was doing.

Did Jonathan know? Of course he knew. He'd said "hurricane party" as a heads-up for stormy weather, not an actual hurricane. Jonathan had his own office with a lovely window and, currently, Jonathan was in a conference room with an even lovelier window. He'd seen the clouds. Daily afternoon showers were common in the late summer.

The concrete and metal stairs echoed as Sophie descended to the Peck and Davilla employee parking level in the garage.

Listening, she didn't hear other cars starting up and hadn't encountered anyone else who might be leaving for a weekend at the beach.

Good. That probably meant a team retreat instead of a big bash. Sophie had heard rumors of a client who might spring for a Super Bowl ad, the Holy Grail of TV advertising. Oh, to be assigned to that creative team. What a career booster, not to mention a jewel in her portfolio. The trick was to stand out and still be considered a team player.

Yeah, yeah. Jonathan *said* he wanted team players, but he'd invited Sophie to the beach house and Aire-An, the ultimate team player, was stuck drawing toothpaste tubes for mock-ups.

Fifteen minutes later, Sophie parked her car on the street in front of the midtown-area townhouse she shared with a couple of roommates. It was in an excellent location with a short commute, but only two bathrooms and a two-car garage. And not so much communal living space.

Her roommates weren't home. Inhaling, Sophie paused to enjoy a rare moment of solitude. And then she started packing.

As soon as Sophie had learned of Jonathan's beach-house parties, she'd shopped for the perfect swimsuit for swimming and the perfect swimsuit for not swimming, as well as appropriate cover-ups. Business beach party—talk about a wardrobe challenge. Now her preparations were going to pay off big-time.

Sophie's goal was to arrive first, or at least early enough to stake out her territory and establish herself as a hostess. As someone in charge. Someone who had her act together. And looked attractive doing it. Sure, it was a throwback to the fifties, but in a way, so was Jonathan. If Sophie had to be the girl who went for coffee, so to speak, then she'd do it.

Speaking of…he'd assigned her steaks and breakfast. Kind of a lot for one person, but she was the newbie, so she'd have to suck it up this time.

But steaks and breakfast for how many people? Was Jonathan planning to grill outside if the weather cleared, or in the kitchen broiler? Did he need propane or charcoal?

Breakfast—did that mean coffee, too? Was there a grinder at the beach house, or should she buy the coffee already ground? Jonathan loved a good cup of coffee, so maybe Sophie should bring her own grinder. And what kind of breakfast? Doughnuts? Or the full bacon-and-eggs weekend feast?

It was four o'clock. Commuter traffic would already be clogging the streets. Sophie still had to shave her legs—clearly no time to book a wax—and apply self-tanner, something she knew from personal experience should *not* be rushed.

Taking a deep, centering breath, she opened her laptop and started a new project list, the first ever to include groceries.

By the time Sophie had touched up her pedicure and packed the car, gusts were jostling every annoying set of wind chimes on the block.

Rain started spitting as she drove to the grocery store. According to the gleeful weathercasters, always happy to have something exciting to report, the storm had jogged north and bands of tropical-storm-force wind and rain would lash the upper Texas coast this weekend.

Well, *that* didn't sound like any fun. From the parking lot of the grocery store, Sophie checked for a follow-up text from Jonathan. Nothing. In fact, nothing from anyone. The party was still on. Okay, then. She pushed open the car door and the wind caught it. Sophie barely stopped it from slamming into the minivan parked alongside. These were some serious gusts. She pushed down her skirt even though she wore her swimsuit beneath it, and hurried into the crowded grocery store to buy steaks and breakfast.

2

ADRIAN DEAN SCOWLED down at the sand beneath the wooden steps leading from the front door of the elevated beach house to a walkway that stopped right at the beach.

He'd come to stand outside on the porch and enjoy the churning ocean and the roiling black clouds and the gusty wind and then, when a crack of lightning had split the horizon, he'd jumped like a girl and dropped the metal pole he'd been disassembling.

On impact, the special, custom-designed bolt had not retracted into the special, custom-designed storage slot the way it was supposed to, but had ejected onto the porch where, driven by the gritty wind, it had rolled through one of the generous gaps in the porch flooring and fallen to the sand.

Even now, blowing sand was hiding the silver glint from Adrian's view. Stupid wind.

"Of course." He exhaled and knew he had to search for the bolt because otherwise, his portable, easy assemble, easy disassemble, prototype home gym would be a useless collection of poles and springs.

Moving quickly, he opened the sliding glass door and put the pole inside with the others, then descended the stairs to ground level. Or rather sand level.

He didn't dither. Because Adrian Dean was not a ditherer—even though he'd just spent five days dithering at the beach.

Over an ad campaign. Just an ad campaign. Or rather two proposals for ad campaigns. Two good, really good proposals. From two really good agencies, one of which owned this very beach house. But two different proposals and he couldn't make up his mind which one to select for the launch of his new portable gym.

Maybe he couldn't pick because he'd decided to go all-out and invest in Super Bowl advertising. It was expensive and he'd never considered it before talking with the Peck and Davilla folks. But they showed him how it made sense to consolidate his advertising budget and go for a big splash. People looked forward to Super Bowl ads, they were discussed and analyzed before and after the game, which resulted in bonus advertising for the companies as well as the ad firms. That's why P&D offered an incredible deal on their fee and assigned their very best to the project.

Adrian was no expert, but he could see the difference between the small local firm he'd been using in Tulsa, where he lived, and P&D. He would never have been able to afford a campaign like the one they proposed plus the expense of broadcast time without the break they'd given him. Definitely worth it.

What he hadn't told P&D was that he'd previously approached Mod Media in Dallas. When he'd let them know why he'd decided to go with P&D, they heard the magic words "Super Bowl" and asked for another meeting. Adrian hesitated, but since he'd increased his budget, he thought it was only fair to see their new pitch.

It was great, but a different great. And now, he didn't know which one to pick.

Adrian stared out at the white caps and the dark clouds moving in. What a metaphor for his state of mind. He could fool himself by thinking he was making a simple marketing choice, but the reality was that if the portable gym took off, his fitness-and-lifestyle company could become huge. Bigger than Adrian could handle by himself. Big enough that Adrian would no longer be able to work personally with clients. So his choice was really whether he wanted to lose the one-on-one interaction he enjoyed in order to grow his business and help more people.

The business was almost to that point now, thanks to his Web site and the regional advertising he'd done the past two years.

On the other hand, this new expensive campaign could be a big bust and cost him his life savings. Yeah. There was that.

P&D figured he was having second thoughts about the Super Bowl–ad cost and had loaned him the beach house so he could take a few days and think. Adrian had been expecting a cottage on stilts, not this…beach mansion.

Did he feel guilty about not telling them they had competition? Mildly. But he also knew this was a psychological move to make him feel obligated to them, so Adrian was calling it even.

Now he scanned the area around his feet, but couldn't see the bolt. Oh, no. That would have been too easy. It was somewhere, beneath the stairs, hidden in the debris, both human and maritime, blowing in from the beach.

People were pigs. He had a new hatred for plastic bottles. And don't get him started on six-pack ring tabs. How could there be a soul left in the universe who hadn't seen pitiful footage of birds and fish caught in the things?

A tumbleweed scratched past his calves. Weren't tumble weeds supposed to be in the desert?

He looked up at the sky as rain suddenly mixed with the wind. "Oh, yes. Let's bring on the rain because poking around in sandy beach trash isn't bad enough."

Adrian had been watching the local weather on the TV ever since he noticed people at neighboring beach houses either leaving or hammering plywood to the window frames.

The forecasters said it was a tropical storm—not even a hurricane. *Yet,* they warned ominously. And maybe not ever. It wasn't supposed to hit Texas—until it bobbled and turned into a big, sloppy storm that might strengthen. Might.

Bobble? Might? Maybe?

No thanks. Adrian had grown up in the Midwest. What he knew were tornadoes which possibly—another wafflely word—could accompany the storm.

So without dithering, he'd called Peck and Davilla and told them he was leaving. He hadn't told them his decision and they hadn't asked. Which was good, because he hadn't decided. Five days and he still couldn't decide.

Adrian stared at the sand, about to dig for a bolt that he needed, literally, to hold his future together. His future was Adrian Dean's Lean Machine. Or Dean's Green Machine, depending on which campaign he chose.

The rain let up and the wind calmed as the cloud band passed. A couple of car doors slammed as yet more surfers whooped and hollered their way to the beach.

In spite of its name, Surfside wasn't a prime surfing area compared to Hawaii or Australia, and the beach was the typical Gulf-coast brown, flecked with bits of tar from the offshore drilling rigs. But he'd enjoyed the break and the privacy and now it was time to get the heck out of Dodge.

Behind the house, another car slowly made its way down the road running parallel to the ocean. More surfers looking for a place to park. They'd better not block him in.

Adrian crouched down, brushed at the sand and shook a ripped Doritos bag, but still couldn't find the bolt.

A car door slammed, closer than before. Footsteps muffled by the sand approached and stopped right in front of him.

"I was sure I was going to be the first one here."

Adrian stared at a pair of hot-pink flip-flops and paler pink toenails, and then lifted his gaze up nicely toned legs. Nicely toned except for those gracilis muscles of the inner thigh. She needed to adjust her workout. He'd start by having her—

"I'd object to you staring up my skirt, except I'm wearing a swimsuit under it." She batted at said skirt, which blocked all points north, including her face. "So don't get all excited because you aren't seeing anything you aren't going to see later."

Adrian quickly stood. After an intro like that, who cared about a missing bolt?

She had pale blue-green eyes with an exotic tilt that kept her from looking too "girl next door-ish" in spite of the ponytail, slightly pug nose and a few freckles.

"I'm Sophie." She thrust out her hand—the one not holding down her skirt. "I don't think we've met."

And what a pity they hadn't. "Adrian Dean," he replied.

Her eyes widened. "The exercise guru?"

She'd actually heard of him. He indulged in a bit of minor preening. "Guru is overstating it a bit, but yes, I run the home-based exercise program." He waited for her to look down at herself, gesture self-consciously and bashfully point out some flaw—real or imagined—and ask him how to fix it. Perhaps those inner-thigh muscles. As it happened, he knew a lot of exercises that would benefit inner thigh muscles. Some were more fun than others.

"So you're here for the party?" she asked.

"I don't know anything about a party."

"You don't?" Clearly surprised, she looked up at the beach house and then back the way she'd come.

"Maybe you're at the wrong beach house?" he suggested

and immediately regretted saying it. For all he knew, she was some opportunistic surfer girl looking for an empty place to crash. A sexy opportunist, though.

"This *is* the Peck and Davilla house?"

He nodded.

"Then I'm at the right place. I work for them." The wind gusted. A strand of hair escaped from her ponytail and she drew it away from her mouth. "It's just that Jonathan didn't mention we were meeting with you."

"He didn't mention that I was meeting with you, either. In fact, I'm leaving."

He couldn't read her expression. In the first place, the wind kept blowing strands of her hair into her face and in the second, she looked both perplexed and anxious.

"Why?" she asked.

He gestured around them. "The weather? Storm warnings?"

"Have the weather guys said it's a hurricane yet?"

"No."

"No biggie, then." As though responding, a stronger gust filled with rain smacked them. Sophie laughed and something within Adrian lightened. She had a great laugh.

"What are you doing under the stairs?" she asked.

"Looking for a bolt I dropped."

"A what?" She cupped her ear against the wind.

"Bolt!" he shouted. "A long tube of silver metal with a hole in each end." He held his fingers three inches apart. "And there should be a cap attached to it."

She bent down. "You mean like this?" Straightening she dropped the bolt into his palm.

"Exactly like that. Thanks!" Relieved, he gestured up the stairs. "Let's head inside."

"I want to get some things out of the car first." Sophie flip-flopped her way around the stairs to the parking area beneath the house.

He considered offering to help her, but honestly, he just wanted to finish packing and leave. So he went inside, refastened the bolt and started to gather the parts of the Lean Machine—or Green Machine—and stopped. His mother had raised him better than to let a woman carry things without offering to help.

He stepped back onto the porch in time to see Sophie struggling with a huge cooler. She was trying to negotiate the stairs without being able to see her feet, which were encased in those useless flip-flops anyway. An accident waiting to happen.

Adrian muttered beneath his breath and met her part way just as the heavens opened. Rain came down in heavy sheets with the wind swirling it in all directions.

Sophie squealed and dashed back to her car. Adrian concentrated on not slipping as he carried the heavy cooler inside.

When he stuck his head back outside, he saw Sophie trying to roll a suitcase across the wet sand. She looked ridiculous with a big, black suitcase at the beach. You brought a duffel bag or back pack to the beach. Everyone knew that.

When she got to the bottom of the stairs, Adrian resigned himself to carrying the thing inside for her. Wordlessly, or more accurately, not saying the words he was thinking aloud, Adrian reached for the suitcase.

Sophie flashed him a smile, brilliant in spite of the rain, but instead of running up the stairs, she flip-flopped back to her car.

"You've got *more* stuff?" he shouted after her.

"This is the last!" She pulled a cardboard box out of the backseat and nudged the car door closed with her hip.

Adrian hurried up the stairs, set the suitcase down and slid the glass door shut as soon as she raced inside.

Sophie dropped the box and turned to him. "Thanks, I—"

There was a metallic *plink* as her foot hit the poles he'd

left inside the door and down she went, taking Adrian with her.

He twisted so he landed flat on his back, Sophie on top of him. As he stared up into those stunned, exotically blue eyes, Adrian reflected that it had been far too long since he'd held a woman in his arms for anything other than exercise spotting. And there weren't too many exercises that required full body contact of the type in which he and Sophie were currently engaged. Right now, he was interested in only one. And the longer she lay on top of him the more interested he became. Amazing how just ten minutes ago, he'd been totally consumed with the question of his future and now Sophie had knocked those thoughts out of his head.

"Ouch," he said softly. A Lean Machine—or Green Machine—pole was beneath his back. *That* was gonna leave a mark.

"Omigosh!" A wet Sophie started wiggling around. Adrian closed his eyes. He had a feeling she was going to leave a mark, too.

"Are you okay?" Her ponytail dripped on his neck.

"I hope so." He shifted off the support pole and she propped herself away from him as she tried to find footing on the wet tile.

Her flip-flop slipped out from under her and she smacked against him. Again. This time his arms clamped around her. It was just reflex. He had excellent reflexes.

"I'm so sorry!" She apologized directly into his neck causing a few good vibrations before lifting her head.

"I'm not." He tried to make his grin convincing because, good vibrations aside, his back did hurt and she'd just scraped his shin. True, it was with a hot-pink rubber flip-flop, but it still stung. Too bad a flip-flop injury didn't exactly make for a story a guy could share in the locker room.

Her skin warmed his and as she breathed, her chest pressed against him. Nice. Wet, but nice. Very nice. He deliberately relaxed the muscles in his arms so her body could settle against his. Her swimsuit left her back bare and before he thought better of it, Adrian spread his fingers over her skin.

And just like that—maybe not *just* like that, but close enough—his hibernating desire yawned and stretched, blinked and said, *Whassup?*

Go back to sleep he ordered it.

But no, it had noticed Sophie. *Heeeelloooo,* it purred.

She stilled, her gaze locked with his. "I am so not flirting with you."

"I so wish you would."

Her expression changed. Actually, it didn't change. It froze.

"Did I say that out loud?" he asked.

"Yes."

"In that case, why aren't you flirting with me? Boyfriend? Husband?"

"Because it's unprofessional."

Did they *have* to be professional?

She levered herself into a sitting position. "Although I must say in a completely sincere and non-flirty way that you have some *serious* abs. I thought I'd hit the floor instead of a human being."

Adrian contracted his abs to sit up. His white shirt was wet and clingy, which set them off nicely, he saw. Sophie, on the other hand, was wearing a swimsuit and looked the same wet as she had dry, except for a messed up ponytail.

She whipped it over her shoulder and tucked stray hair behind her ears. "What did I trip over anyway?"

"Poles to my home gym. I was disassembling it." He stood and held out a hand to help her up.

"Thanks." She braced herself until she was upright. Then she casually stripped off her wet skirt.

That got his attention, as women undressing tended to do.

He'd momentarily forgotten that the skirt was only covering a swim suit and got a sexy little zing. But hey, as long as they were dispensing with wet clothes...Adrian peeled off his shirt. Might as well display the abs. He'd worked for them. Now let them work for him.

"What a mess." Sophie tossed her wet skirt in a corner and looked all around them. "We have to dry the floor before the others get here or people will be falling all over the... holy moly!"

Sophie had noticed Adrian and his abs, which he'd expertly displayed. *Yeah, you don't see these too often. Still want to keep things professional?*

"You're like...plastic man." She approached him. "Are those real?" As she spoke, she poked her finger at his stomach.

He flinched. "Yes, they're real!"

Sophie glanced up at him and then leaned closer and squinted.

"What are you doing?"

"Looking for surgery scars."

"You're not going to find any!" He wished he hadn't taken off his shirt, even though it was wet. Balling it up, he tossed it toward her skirt. Too bad the rest of his clothes were already packed in his car.

"It's just..." She gestured mutely. "You look so perfect. The chest...proportion wise...and the length of your torso—not too long and not too short and barrelly. Is that a word? You know what I mean. Your torso tapers nicely to your waist." She nodded to herself. "Well done, you."

Adrian stared at her. *He* was usually the one to analyze another's body shape. And then only when asked. At least aloud.

"I heard you were going to appear in your own ads. Now I see why. You're your own best advertisement."

"I'm considering it." She'd said he looked perfect. When

a woman admired him, an invitation, either subtle or blatant, usually followed. Adrian responded with a standard regretful refusal that left them both feeling good.

He gazed down at Sophie, with her wet hair and her interesting eyes and her swimsuit-clad body, and felt neither regret nor a refusal.

He felt unprofessional. He smiled.

Head tilted, Sophie stepped back and examined his face. "Yeah, some makeup and good lighting—maybe putty on the cheekbones to emphasize shadows—and even your head will work."

His smile faltered. "Gee, thanks." Putty? *Putty?*

"Hey, it's a good thing. It means you can do personal appearances, if it's necessary. Otherwise, we'd Photoshop a new head for you in the print ads."

Adrian could think of nothing to say. Nothing. There was no invitation for him to decline—or accept. This was not the way it was supposed to work.

Sophie was making him feel, maybe not *insecure,* but certainly less confident in his appearance. Not that he expected every woman he met to fall into his arms. Which, incidentally, she already had.

Sophie slid her foot into the flip-flop that had skidded beneath the kitchen bar dividing the living area. "Do you happen to know where they keep the mop around here? Between the wet sand and…what's wrong?"

"I—nothing."

"Something. You look weird."

"Maybe because I'm not wearing makeup or putty on my cheeks."

"You'd probably have putty on your chin, too."

Adrian instinctively rubbed his chin.

Sophie laughed. "Kidding. Sort of." She knuckled his chin. "It's a perfectly fine chin just the way it is."

"Yeah, but what about the rest of my face?" Adrian knew

that outside the gym he wasn't a first-tier looker—the guys women immediately noticed when they cased a room. But he got plenty of attention. No complaints. And inside the gym, well. He ruled inside the gym.

"It's a good face. A solid face."

Good? Solid?

She smiled. "That's a compliment."

"Oh." Lucky thing she'd told him. "Well…thanks."

Sophie stood close enough for him to smell the flowery shampoo she'd used mixed with the salty sea weedy smell he'd been breathing for the last week. Heat radiated from her damp skin. Or maybe that was his damp skin. Whatever. There was radiation going on.

Awareness flowed through him, flipping on switches, starting the engines, rallying the troops.

This will do you no good. We're leaving, he told his now fully-awake desire.

In the rain? Do you really want to drive in the rain? Think of the traffic going through Houston. The wrecks. The flooding.

Sophie picked up the box she'd brought and headed to the kitchen. There was a sexy jiggle to her glutes that women paid him to get rid of. Why? That little jiggle said "woman." That little jiggle made him want to grab her bottom and squeeze.

Now why would you want to waste your time staring at a line of cars when you could stare at Sophie? his desire whispered insidiously.

Adrian felt himself being swayed. The weather was truly awful. And Sophie was truly not.

"Found it!" she sang and held up an old sponge mop.

You should stay to help her clean up the floor.

It was the desire talking. But he *should* help. He'd been here a week and hadn't mopped once. She said people were arriving. So okay. He'd stay. And it wasn't because of desire. It was because of the weather.

That would be the moment that the rain audibly slackened.

Sophie's gaze flitted to the window. "The rain has let up. We're between the bands of thunderstorms. Now's the time to pack up your—" she gestured to the partially disassembled gym "—exercise thing. That is if you still intend to skip out on one of Jonathan's awesome beach parties."

"Um, yeah." Not the most enthusiastic invitation he'd ever heard.

Feeling deflated, Adrian picked up the canvas duffel designed to hold the gym. Currently, the fabric was navy blue. He liked navy. But if he went with Dean's Green Machine, it would be green, of course. Green was okay, but it was no navy.

Sophie's suit was navy with a white band outlining the top. The whole thing fastened around her neck, exposing her strong shoulders. It was all one piece instead of a bikini. Classy, sexy. And navy. Had he mentioned navy?

He stared across the room at Sophie in the kitchen as she put away the food and supplies that had been in the box while she waited for him to move the poles.

Slowly, Adrian took apart the last two pieces and folded the seat until it was flat against the bench part. He put this, the largest part, into the duffel first. Next came the longest poles, but they were wet from the sand and water he and Sophie had tracked in. He really should wipe them off before packing them away. There were paper towels in the kitchen. Where Sophie was.

He saw her pull a large white plastic jar from the cabinet and frown as she read the label.

"Adrian Dean's Power Protein Mix." She looked over at him. "Yours, I'm assuming?"

"Yeah, thanks. I'd forgotten it."

"'Mix a quarter cup with twelve ounces water, shake or blend and drink in place of breakfast and lunch. Adrian Dean's Power Protein contains all the nutrients needed to fuel your body for peak performance, both physically and mentally.'" She unscrewed the top and sniffed, immediately making a face. "Is this all you eat?"

"I eat soy bars for dinner. It's part of the nutrition plan I'm developing."

"No *wonder* you're so grumpy." She set the jar on the counter and carried the mop out of the kitchen.

Grumpy? He hadn't been grumpy. He'd helped her carry stuff. He'd cushioned her fall. She'd *injured* him and he hadn't complained. When had he been grumpy?

"I thought you'd be finished by now." Sophie stared down at the poles. "Isn't that supposed to be easy to assemble and disassemble?"

"It is, but how do you know?"

"It's obvious." She gestured. "And I studied the agency's campaign notes."

"You're working on my ad?"

"Not specifically. I mean, I haven't been assigned to it, but..." She looked up at him, and he could see her hesitate. "But the rumor is you're considering a Super Bowl ad." Her eyes searched his.

"I might be, if the ad is good enough."

She exhaled. "That's huge."

"I *know*."

"Expensive."

"I know."

"So...what's the ad?"

"I don't know."

3

HE DIDN'T KNOW? HE hadn't decided on a campaign? Sophie concentrated on keeping her breathing even and her face professionally interested. If Adrian couldn't decide on the advertising that meant nothing had grabbed him yet. And if none of P&D's proposals had grabbed him, he wasn't likely to plunk down a couple million bucks for a Super Bowl spot. Before production costs.

Jonathan was unaware of Adrian's lack of enthusiasm for the campaigns he'd seen. Sophie would bet her job on it. In fact, that's what she was about to do.

Hadn't she prepared for an opportunity? Hadn't she been chasing after opportunities and flinging herself in their path? She'd collided with them. Been steamrolled by them. Been tricked by them. She'd let them slip out of her grasp. She'd grabbed and missed them. And she'd blown them. But she'd never *ignored* an opportunity.

She'd never encountered an opportunity with a body like Adrian's, either. All that physical perfection was distracting, especially since he'd taken off his shirt. But he was a client—or at least a potential client. So until the others arrived, she'd work harder at not being distracted by his ideal shoulder-to-waist ratio and chest made for nuzzling. Or the way he'd felt beneath her body when she'd fallen on him. Twice. Or the gentle sweep of his fingers on her back—the memory made her skin prickle even now.

Adrian was still talking. *Pay attention, Sophie.*

"That's why I was staying here a few days—to decompress and think. Jonathan told me to take a week and relax. Soak up the sun. Listen to the waves."

Sophie's gaze drifted to his chest as she flashed on an image of a gleaming, bronzed Adrian soaking up the sun and listening to the waves. Wow. Keeping focused was hard. This must be what men went through when talking to women with huge boobs.

"Empty my mind and the answer would come to me, he said." Adrian grimaced. "Didn't happen. But you know, the second day, I fell asleep on the veranda—luckily in the shade—and slept for, like, six hours and then came inside and slept for nine more. And the day after that, I read a book. A whole book. Start to finish. No interruptions."

"That's great." Sophie hoped it was great. It didn't sound great that Adrian was into physical fitness, yet was such a stress bunny. With a tendency to babble. That she found rather charming instead of annoying the way she usually reacted to babbling. Such was the power of Adrian's body. With a body like that, he could babble all he wanted to.

She was objectifying him. Oh, this was not good.

Looking away from him, she swiped the mop over the tile, scooting the poles aside.

Adrian didn't seem to notice. "I needed this week, but when the storm headed here, I could feel myself tighten up again. I know I've got to tell Jonathan something, but I have no idea what."

Then Sophie would talk him through it. Brainstorm with him. Hand hold him into committing. After that, how could Jonathan *not* put her on the ad campaign? And with such a highly visible project, she knew he'd be leading the team himself. He'd hear her ideas directly and not filtered through Ross, and by filtered, she meant leaving out her name.

If she could help Adrian, then they'd both benefit.

"When I get too close to a project, I like to get a fresh perspective." She stood the mop upright. "Since I don't know anything about what you've been shown, maybe it'll help if you talk to me."

"Sounds good." He nodded several times. "Yes. Thanks."

Look at the guy. His jaw was clenched and he held a world of tension in those gorgeous shoulders.

"First, why don't you finish putting away the machine—what do you call it?"

"That depends on which ad campaign I go with. It's either Adrian Dean's Lean Machine or Dean's Green Machine." He had a wild expression in his eyes.

"You don't have to decide right this minute," Sophie assured him hastily. He was ready to blow. "Honestly, I don't know how you can think at all. When was the last time you ate real food?"

"I eat real food. I fuel my body with all the nutrients—"

"You eat reconstituted powdered chemicals. I'm talking about real food." Sophie carried the mop into the kitchen and rinsed it out. "When was the last time you ate a thick, juicy, well-marbled, medium-rare, charcoal-grilled steak?"

"Red meat?" He looked horrified.

"Or pink, depending on how cooked you like it."

"Do you have any idea what beef does to your body?"

"Yes. Add a salad and a glass of red wine and I'm a happy girl."

"Your arteries aren't happy."

"My brain is happy. It thinks clearly. It makes decisions. And right now, it's decided to broil a couple of the primo steaks I've brought and feed you dinner."

"Sophie, I don't think that's a good idea." But he looked tempted.

"It's an excellent idea, even without charcoal. Your failure to recognize a good idea is yet another example of brain malfunction caused by lack of food." She opened the fridge and withdrew a butcher paper–wrapped bundle. The others could cook for themselves when they arrived. It wasn't as though Jonathan was going to grill outdoors tonight and Sophie was hungry.

She continued to stare into the fridge. No veggies, just condiments of an indeterminate age and the breakfast food she'd brought. "Adrian? Would you check in the living room cabinets to see if you can find any wine? There's bound to be some around here." Peering at him from behind the fridge door she asked, "Or do you drink?"

He still stood in the same spot. "Occasionally."

Well, that was a relief because Sophie really, really wanted a glass of wine and she really, really didn't want to drink if the client didn't.

Adrian stared at her, obviously not completely convinced to stay. Sophie threw him a bright smile and ducked behind the door again, fingers crossed.

Moments later, she heard him open the doors in the cabinets beneath the bookshelves. "You said you prefer red?"

She exhaled. "Yes, please."

When he brought the wine over to the kitchen bar, Sophie handed him a corkscrew and foil cutter and watched him concentrate on opening the bottle. He looked more relaxed now that he wasn't thinking about costly ad campaigns.

Sophie seasoned the steaks and preheated the broiler. She hadn't brought any side dishes because she assumed they'd been assigned to someone else. Adrian had spent the week eating his protein powder which meant the fridge had nothing she could scavenge. Breaking into the breakfast fruit, she sliced a cantaloupe and sprinkled a few blueberries onto the plates as Adrian pulled the cork.

Sophie set two goblets on the bar and listened to the happy glugging of wine from a full bottle as Adrian poured. "Good choice," she sighed after taking her first sip. "P&D probably stocked the place for you. I'm glad there are leftovers to tide us over until Jonathan gets here."

"About that." Adrian glanced at his watch. "It's getting really late."

"Just eight o'clock. And he was in a meeting. If you consider the drive from Houston, the traffic and the weather, it's not late at all." Sophie took another sip. Adrian was still shirtless and now that he'd dried off enough to lose the shine, he didn't look so much like plastic man as underwear model man. This part of his body would need no retouching.

Speaking of touching...Sophie learned something new about herself—male underwear models apparently were her type. Yes, she was as surprised as anybody, but honestly, an abtastic torso in three dimensions was so much better than a two-dimensional photo. Intellectually, she'd known that. But when faced with Adrian in the flesh, flesh that was standing less than three feet away...zowie. She'd had no idea she was so visual. Adrian hit all the primal female programming: find strong mate. Have strong babies.

The urge to walk around the bar and run her hands all over his torso was so powerful her fingertips actually tingled. She wanted to feel muscles flexing beneath warm, male flesh. She'd been pressed up against that torso. Why, oh, why hadn't she savored the moment? She needed another moment. Moments. Lots and lots of moments.

Sophie tightened her tingling fingers around her wineglass and drank a heck of a lot more than a sip. Keeping things strictly professional was going to be difficult.

To cover up the amount of time she'd been staring, she

said, "I can see all your muscles outlined. You could be show-and-tell for an anatomy class."

In the process of setting her wine on the counter, Sophie became aware that Adrian just stood there, holding his glass. One might say he was posing. Her gaze flicked up to his face. One would be right. Sophie caught the tiny curve of his lips. Not quite a smile, but enough to tell her that having women admire his body was familiar territory to him. He expected it. He'd noticed her scrutiny. And he'd enjoyed it.

Okay, so she'd admired him. She was human. She was female. What was he waiting for—applause? "I'm starting the steaks. If you're planning to stay, now would be a good time to get a dry shirt out of your car. I hear the wind starting to gust again."

As she turned away, Sophie saw a puzzled surprise cross his face. *Yeah, that's right. Go put on a shirt, bud.* She wasn't going to allow a nice manly body to distract her from the mission. And no, she reminded herself firmly, the nice manly body was *not* the mission. Business was the mission.

Sophie slipped the steaks under the broiler as she heard the glass doors slide open and closed. Then she dug through her suitcase until she found the sarong she'd planned to use as a cover-up tomorrow. Too bad. She needed it now. The more clothes between her and Mr. Universe, the better.

Speaking of, Adrian pulled open the door just as Sophie flipped the steaks. He'd been out there awhile.

"Is your cell getting a signal?" he asked. "I wanted to make a call, but couldn't find a good spot."

"It was earlier." Sophie dug in her purse and flipped her phone open. "No service for me, either. But that's not surprising. We're on the fringes out here." No messages had come through from Jonathan. But how long had she been out of the cell-service area?

"The wind has really picked up," Adrian commented.

"I hear it," Sophie said. Carefully avoiding looking at him, she went back into the kitchen. "I'm going to light candles in case the power goes out." Because she sure didn't want him to think she was making a romantic dinner. She was feeding him so he could think about the ad campaign.

"Good idea." He carried a bag into the master bedroom. It was probably where he'd been sleeping. There was an entire second floor with another living area and a wraparound balcony and kitchenette. Lots more bedrooms, so no weird awkwardness about sleeping arrangements when everybody else got here.

Sophie straightened up the kitchen and was hanging their wet clothes in the laundry when she heard Adrian call.

"Sophie?"

She came out only to find him still shirtless. *Think goals. Think long-term career goals.*

"Would you take my picture before I eat?" He handed her a digital camera.

She gave him a look before examining the camera.

"No, I am not a narcissist. I've been following my own program for three weeks. I intended to give it a month, but twenty-one days will be enough. I have before pictures—"

"Tell me they're not the ones I'm seeing in the camera." She clicked through them.

"Well, yeah."

"Your before pictures are other people's fantasy pictures."

He smiled briefly. "You see this muscle definition?"

She rolled her eyes.

"Seriously. After I eat that steak and have a glass of wine or two, you won't see it. My body will retain water and soften the definition."

"Are you saying you'll bloat? Because *I* know bloat and there's no way. No. Way."

He laughed and she realized it was the first time she'd heard him do so. "It's a body-builder thing."

"I thought you were targeting the home market. Regular people, not body builders."

"I am. I'm adapting some of the body builders' strategies for everyday fitness."

"Everyday Fitness." Sophie stared off into the middle distance. "That sounds pretty good, actually. Except, I'm sorry, but on what planet is drinking powdered gunk considered practical for normal people?"

He gave her a sheepish and unexpectedly appealing grin. "I'm rethinking that. The steaks smell great."

Steaks? Oh. Right. "So you want pictures before you break your diet."

"Yes. I can always market it as an anti-bloat diet. You can be one of my testers."

His grin no longer appealed. "Why *thank* you. You're too kind."

Adrian caught the tone in her voice. "You're the one who brought up bloating issues."

Sophie narrowed her eyes. "No…I think that was you."

"C'mon, Sophie, you're a beautiful woman."

He said she was beautiful and he said it as though it was an obvious fact. She liked that. Liked it a lot. Liked in a way that twanged her heartstrings.

Unfortunately, he continued. "With some exerci—"

"Stop." She held up a hand. "'Sophie, you're a beautiful woman.' And stop."

"Yes, but—"

"Stop."

"What I meant—"

"Stop."

Adrian sucked his breath through his teeth. "I can't figure out what you think I'm going to say that's so wrong."

Sophie leveled a look at him. "That's because you haven't been eating properly. Now be quiet and pose."

After adjusting the lighting, such as it was, they cleared space so Adrian could stand in front of a blank wall. Sophie took pictures of Adrian inhaling. Adrian flexing. Adrian from the side. Adrian's back. He even had a great back. And the little stretchy pair of trunks he wore showed off buns of steel.

So he had a great body. Was that *all* she could think about?

"How's the light? Can you see the muscle definition okay?" he asked.

"Oh, yes." Sophie wiped her hands against the wrap she wore and propped her elbows on the back of the sofa to steady the camera.

A few seconds later, the timer for the steaks dinged. Thank goodness because staring at Adrian was making her hands sweat and shake. She hoped the pictures wouldn't be blurry.

Adrian walked toward her in his little stretchy trunks. Sophie saw him in slow motion. Thigh muscles bunched and released. His torso swiveled gently. Swaying arms emphasized defined shoulders.

And all she could do was stand there, unblinking, and try not to drool. Forget hiding her response to him. The best strategy was to acknowledge that she, like most women, appreciated a good-looking male, treat it as a natural reaction, but not take it any further.

Deep inside her something whimpered, but she slapped it into silence. Still, she came close to dropping the camera as she handed it back to him.

Adrian smiled down at her as he took the camera from her damp, shaky fingers. "Sophie?"

"Hmm?"

He waited until she met his eyes. A few beats passed

before his gaze slowly drifted to her mouth, around the contours of her face, paused at her mouth again, and returned to her eyes.

"You're a beautiful woman." And he stopped.

4

AND HOW HAD SOPHIE responded to his deliberate, unmistakable, provocative, I-find-you-incredibly-attractive, unignorable look? Which, incidentally, had been in response to her I-want-you-so-bad-I-can-barely-control-myself zombie stare?

By ignoring it. He'd told her she was beautiful and stopped just the way she'd wanted him to. Instead of melting into his arms, she'd squeaked out a thank-you, and then served him his first steak in three years.

"Blueberries are full of antioxidants," she told him when he'd stared at his plate for several long moments.

"I know." And in a minute, he'd eat one.

"Is your meat too rare?" As she spoke, Sophie cut into hers and red juices ran onto the white plate.

"No, it's fine." He swallowed to ease the tightness in his throat. "It smells great." And it did in a fatty, salty way.

The thing was, he did not know how his stomach was going to react to regular food after twenty-one days. And if it did not react well, he would rather Sophie didn't have that image in her head. Such images weren't conducive to romantic overtures, should he want to make another one. And he was considering it. She liked the way he looked.

Until her trancelike stare as he'd walked toward her a few minutes ago, he hadn't been completely sure.

He liked the way she looked, too, but he also liked her. A lot, actually, for the amount of time he'd known her. The problem was that she had a point about not muddying the professional and personal waters.

Anyway, according to her, people were supposed to descend upon them at any moment, but it seemed strange that P&D had planned a party and not told him. He was supposed to be gone by now, so it really wasn't any of his business. Unless Jonathan had planned the party before Adrian decided to leave, but his assistant hadn't said anything when Adrian had called this afternoon. And now it was what? Almost nine o'clock? Except for clusters of tiny lights on the off-shore drilling rigs, it was solidly black outside. He could hear the wind, a rushing sound punctuated with occasional bumps against the windows. He hoped anyone traveling in this mess arrived safely.

But in the meantime, there was a plate of food sitting in front of him. Better start with the blueberries. Cautiously, he speared one with his fork and enjoyed the burst of flavor. He ate a few more before he became aware of Sophie watching him.

She set down her silverware and leaned across the table. "Cut a piece off right there." She pointed to the steak.

Adrian hesitated.

"Go on."

So he did. The knife slid through the meat as though it were butter, appropriate because tenderness equaled fat. But he wasn't going to think about that. He was committed to eating the steak. At least some of it. He opened his mouth.

"Wait. Smell it." She demonstrated, inhaling deeply.

He mimicked her.

"Now slowly bring the fork to your lips and set it on your tongue. Taste before chewing. Savor."

The blueberries had burst, but the steak was a flavor explosion. Adrian tasted salt and smoky bits of the charred edge first, and then the rest of the seasoning she'd used rolled across his tongue. Underneath was the earthy taste of a quality steak. He swallowed and exhaled. Wow.

"Good?" She smiled a sensual, knowing smile.

"Great." What else was great was the way Sophie looked in the candlelight just then. Shadows played across her shoulders and neck and her lips glistened.

But it was her eyes that drew him in. Intelligence, he liked that. Less so the amusement, since he figured it was directed at him. Interest, certainly, and earlier, awareness which she'd since hidden. So what else was hiding in those deceptively clear blue eyes?

"The steak's not bad for sticking it under a broiler." Straightening, Sophie took a bite of her own steak and closed her eyes as she chewed. "Mmm."

She meant "mmm" about the steak, but Adrian felt the vibrations deep in his gut. It had been way too long since he'd heard a woman "mmm." And when he had, she hadn't been "mmming" about food.

He watched Sophie while he ate more steak. She was right. He could feel his brain focusing already. And it was focused on her.

Sophie opened her eyes and caught him staring at her. She stared back. For a timeless moment, Adrian knew that Sophie was thinking about him in a way that had nothing to do with food. He hoped she realized he was totally fine with that.

And then—*right* at the very moment Adrian was ready drop his fork, hold out his hand, draw Sophie to her feet and lead her into the bedroom, professionalism be damned, something blew against the front windows. The rattling thump made her blink and the moment passed.

"So...I get 'Lean Machine,' but where did 'Green Machine' come from?" she asked him.

Adrian didn't want to discuss exercise equipment. His mind was fueled by good beef and relaxed by wine and very focused right now. Wasting that kind of focus was just not right.

But Sophie's eyes had lost that sleepy sexy look, so Adrian forced himself to answer her question. "The machine is earth-friendly since it's a home-based exercise system. People don't drive to a gym so no car emissions pollute the air. Less of a carbon footprint."

"Piggybacking on the whole going green thing." She nodded thoughtfully. "But the name doesn't say anything about what your product is. Green Machine—what's that? Lawn care? A college football team? I don't think of fitness equipment when I hear 'Green Machine.'"

Adrian didn't, either, but the ad guys were professionals. They knew marketing. "The thinking was that I could use the color in the branding. It rhymes with Dean."

Sophie made a face. "You don't need a color. *You're* the brand. You're the Dean of Lean."

"Hey, that's pretty good."

"I think so." She grinned. "Tell me about the other ad pitch."

And so he did. Sophie picked it apart while they finished eating and brainstormed with him while they cleaned up.

"These campaigns sound as though their message is coming from the people who created them and not you. And by message, I'm talking about the one other than the 'buy me' message," she told him.

Something clicked into place for Adrian. He'd been scrubbing the burned bits off the broiler pan while Sophie dried and put away their plates and he just stopped and stared at her. "*My* message."

"Yeah." She closed the cabinet door. "The first campaign's

message is 'be earth-friendly while you exercise' and the other's is 'lose weight so you'll look good.'"

"My program isn't about looking good!" He exhaled in frustration.

"Ooo, as a message, 'exercise and deprive yourself and forget about looking good' isn't going to fly."

"You're right." He gave a short laugh and started scrubbing again. "But if it takes selling the 'we can make you look good' aspect of my program, then so be it."

"Not necessarily." She leaned against the counter. "What is your message?"

"I have no idea."

"Sure you do. Something drew you to health and fitness in the first place. And then you needed something and couldn't find it, so you developed your own—" she gestured toward the duffel "—exercise thingy. And now..." She gestured toward him.

"And now what?"

"And now you tell me what those 'somethings' were. How did you get into the exercise business?"

"I played sports in school and enjoyed learning how to keep my body in peak condition. And later, I wanted to share what I learned with others."

"Great. Remember that. It'll make good ad copy. So why did you start your own program?"

"My sister."

"Because...?"

"Because she's a pain in the ass."

"Not good copy."

He grinned, feeling calmer for the first time in days. Weeks, if he was honest. There was something about Sophie that just...there was something about Sophie. Something unexpected and it appealed to him in a big way.

"Megan's a geriatric specialist," he told her. "She's always complaining that a lot of the health issues she sees in her patients could have been prevented if they'd made modest lifestyle changes when they were younger. It makes her *insane.* And really obnoxious because she lectures people."

"Good to know. We'll keep her off camera."

Adrian nodded. "Don't get me wrong—I love her, but she has *no* people skills except with her patients. She's been that way ever since she did her rotation in geriatrics. She came home and literally pulled Dad off the sofa and told him to jog around the block. Then she force fed Mom calcium."

Sophie laughed. "So what did she do to you?"

"Made me a believer." Adrian rinsed the broiler and handed it to her. "I was working as a sports trainer. She asked if I would develop a simple exercise routine for her patients. I did, but it was more appropriate for an athlete coming off an injury because that's what I knew. So she made me come with her when she visited her retirement-home patients—kind of a crash course in geriatrics. All day long, she pointed out stuff like the guy with the bad knees who'd worked on the third floor of a building. If all he'd done was take the stairs every day instead of the elevator, he would have weighed less and his muscles would have been stronger and his joints wouldn't have taken such a beating and so on."

Sophie nodded as she put away the broiler and beckoned him to the dining table.

"It was the same with practically every patient. By the end of the day, I was totally onboard. It's amazing how just little changes in the way we live now make a big difference later in our quality of life."

Sophie grabbed his arm. "That's your message!"

Adrian was jolted out of his story by the excited expression on her face and the warmth of her hand on his arm.

"It is, isn't it?" She still gripped his arm and gave it a little tug when he didn't answer right away.

And he didn't answer because he was fighting the urge

to lean in and kiss her. She looked so bright and happy and she was touching him and there wasn't room in his head for both Sophie and whatever he'd been talking about.

"Little changes now, big results later—something like that, right?" She seemed to realize that she was gripping his arm and released it.

He could still feel the imprint of her hand. "Um, yeah."

"So then what?" She was honestly interested, not faking it out of politeness or professional necessity.

Genuine interest was incredibly attractive, Adrian discovered as he told her about his sister's frustration when she couldn't get through to patients' families. "And you know, she's right, but she alienates people when she goes on and on. In her mind, she's showing them living proof that they're headed in the same direction unless they make some changes, but people either don't believe her or make excuses."

"Giving up food for powdered chemicals is not a modest lifestyle adjustment." They were sitting at the dining table with the ad-presentation folders spread open around them and Sophie pointed to a page showing different versions of labels for his protein powder.

Adrian exhaled. "I got a little side-tracked. You know, the personal training pays the bills, but you're right. I should stick to my core goals. Simple. Accessible. Appealing. And online support."

"Okay." Sophie flipped over the piece of paper and began writing on the back. "Let's start there."

Adrian didn't know how long he and Sophie strategized before he got the idea that she should put together the exercise equipment so she could see how easy it was to assemble.

"People say they can't get to the gym—I'm bringing the gym to them. They don't have room? It fits in a duffel bag. Too complicated, too time consuming to put together? Try it. I'll time you."

"And then you're going to make me use it, aren't you?" Sophie grumbled.

"Oh, you'll *want* to use it," he assured her. "Exercise is good for you. How could you not want your body to feel great?"

"I can think of many other ways my body can feel great," she muttered.

"I can help you with those, too." His offer was totally sincere. He couldn't remember the last time he'd felt this much sincerity. They might be ignoring it, but the attraction was definitely there, simmering just below the surface. They were so in sync mentally. Didn't she wonder how it would be physically?

Sophie didn't even glance at him. "That's the steak talking." Sinking to the floor, she read the directions printed on the inside of the storage bag.

"Hey, don't bother with those. Assembly is so simple you don't need any instructions."

Without looking away, Sophie said, "I am not mechanically adept. Trust me, this is not false modesty." She held out her hand. "I require wine."

SOPHIE HOPED HE remembered her help when he discussed the campaign with Jonathan. *I want Sophie on the team. We work really well together. She so gets me and what I'm trying to do. You know, she even*—"Ow!"—*pinched the skin between her thumb and finger right in the most painful spot and acted as though it was nothing. She barely noticed because she was concentrating so hard on learning how to assemble my stupid home gym.* Or words to that effect.

"Ow-ow-ow-ow-ow-ow!"

"Let me see it." Adrian sat next to her and held out his hand.

"No." He'd think she was being a big baby, even though it did hurt.

"Sophie…" He reached for her hand, but Sophie just wanted to get on with assembling the stupid machine.

"You're bleeding."

"What?" Surprised, she stopped struggling before Adrian could react and he pulled her hand into his chest, leaving a smear of blood on his white shirt.

It was a duplicate of the one he'd worn before, white knit with the Adrian Dean logo embroidered on the breast in navy. Yeah, whatever worked for him. And it did, actually. Or it did without the blood.

"I'm sorry," she said.

"I should apologize to you." He lifted the hem of his shirt and pressed it against the base of her thumb. "Obviously, the bolt has got to be redesigned."

His hands were warm and he seemed genuinely concerned. And he was using his shirt to stop her bleeding. What a guy.

Actually, yes. What a guy.

Ever since she'd tripped and landed on top of him—because he'd deliberately positioned himself to take the fall—Sophie had tried to remain detached.

The man was seriously hot. The problem with seriously hot guys was that they were aware of it. And the problem with *that* was some men felt it was enough when they and their hotness decided to favor a woman with their attention. Sort of an "I've noticed you. Aren't you lucky?" attitude.

Sophie had gone for the hot guy with the sense of entitlement before. Okay, several times. But not this time. Adrian was a *client*. He was off-limits. How could he take her seriously if she fell into bed with him as easily as any other woman? How was he supposed to know that at some point during the hours they'd been talking, she'd become attracted to more than his body? Just her luck that Adrian had brains and brawn all tied together with a big off-limits bow.

While all this was going through her mind, he was

regarding her questioningly, as he held her hand and looked hot. The nerve.

"I'll live." She tugged her hand away. "You need to rinse out your shirt or it'll stain."

"Forget the shirt. Let me see the damage."

"I can't forget the shirt. My blood is on the shirt."

"So I'll ditch the shirt." He pulled it over his head. "Let's go clean the cut."

"It's more of a mangle than a cut."

He stood and helped her up. "Are you trying to make me feel worse?"

"No." She was trying to avoid looking at his chest again. She just could not keep clothes on the man. Maybe it was a sign.

The lights suddenly dimmed, blinked and then went out altogether. Without Sophie's candles, the place would have been completely dark. Instead, the room had become cozily intimate.

Talk about a sign. She was with a total hunk who owned a successful business and seemed like a genuinely good guy. They were alone in a luxurious beach house during a storm, which meant nobody was going anywhere for hours. The lights were out, candles were lit, and, oh yes, the hunk was already half-undressed. Yeah. She didn't need a neon arrow, here.

No, she needed a neon sign that blinked Client.

Too bad the electricity was out.

Now that the air conditioning and the refrigerator motors were off, the moaning howl of the wind filled the house.

"Listen to that," Adrian said. "Wind is always described as roaring or howling, and it really does sound that way."

"I hear a little shrieking mixed in, too." How could Sophie have missed the passing time and the worsening weather? Talking with Adrian, that's how.

Wind gusts stressed the windows to the breaking point

and the whole house creaked. "We should lower the storm shutters," Sophie said.

Adrian headed toward the kitchen. "There's a list of instructions taped to the inside of one of the cabinets."

Picking up her wineglass, Sophie followed him. His torso gleamed, *gleamed* by candlelight. She sighed and the candle on the bar wavered.

"Uh oh. The storm shutters are electrically powered."

"I was afraid of that." While Adrian read the storm-prep instructions, Sophie lit the propane lantern she'd found with the emergency supplies in the laundry-room closet.

"The shutters can be disconnected and manually lowered, but we'll have to go outside to do it," Adrian told her.

Sophie groaned. "The upstairs windows will be okay, but we should protect the windows on this level for sure. The danger is from all the debris blowing around. Plastic lounge chairs, sand toys, barbeque implements—that kind of thing will go flying. I'd rather lower the shutters now than deal with broken windows later."

"Then let's get to it. Grab the lantern." Adrian strode to the door.

Wind and rain slapped at them as they yanked out the shutters and lowered them. Even with the lantern, Sophie couldn't see and struggled with the locks.

Adrian finished the two on his side of the veranda and stood sheltering her from the worst of the needlelike rain as he fastened hers, as well. And then he continued to shield her as they made their way around to the back of the house and finished lowering shutters.

Sophie expected to be annoyed with herself for not pulling her own weight. Instead, she felt girlie and protected.

And turned on.

Yes. There was that. Being outside with Adrian while Mother Nature threw a temper tantrum was exciting and raw and primal. Man and woman working together against the elements. Man, brave and strong. Woman, good for holding a flashlight.

Once they were back inside and had secured the glass door against the wind and rain, they both leaned with their backs against it, breathing heavily. Sophie's skin tingled from the stinging rain.

"Wow," Adrian exhaled.

"Wow is right." Sophie closed her eyes.

Behind them, the wind roared and the rain scraped against the shuttered windows. The sound was muted now. Except for the candles and the lantern, they might have been in a cave.

Sophie could hear their breathing slow, at least until Adrian turned his head. She kept her eyes closed, but imagined his gaze on her shoulders and chest, dipping along the severely tailored and fitted neckline of her suit, the one that was meant to suggest, rather than reveal.

Sophie thought of a few suggestions, and as she did, inhaled and opened her eyes and met Adrian's burning stare. She was pretty sure her stare was burning right back. And there went her heart, thudding heavily.

She shouldn't look at a man that way unless she planned on following through. Part of her wanted to follow through *right now.*

Adrian raised his hand toward her face. The part of Sophie that remembered her career goals and how hard she'd worked toward them caused her to flinch the tiniest bit.

Adrian lowered his hand and looked away. "We're dripping all over the floor. I'll get the mop," he said roughly.

The mop was propped by the back kitchen entrance where she'd left it. When he returned, he swiped at the puddle by the door, and then very slowly, and very deliberately, set the mop against the wall.

Drawing his hands to his hips, he said, "I don't think anyone else is going to show up tonight."

Sophie's mouth was dry—the only thing about her that was. "I don't think so, either."

"And I'm not driving anywhere in that mess out there."

"Me, either." Sophie tried to swallow. Tried to put distance between them.

But not very hard.

"It's just you and me. Here. Together. Alone." He took the tiniest of steps toward her. Testing.

Sophie wanted to step back or to the side or anywhere that would let him know she wasn't that kind of girl. But all she managed was an unconvincing sway.

"No power. Nothing to do." Another step. "Except listen to the wind and the rain for hours and hours…"

He'd moved into Sophie's personal space.

Now was the time to step away from the client. Truthfully, the time was a few seconds ago, but now would work, too.

Adrian lifted his hand and Sophie swayed, this time toward him. "I'm not that kind of girl."

Adrian traced his fingers down a strand of wet hair. There were a lot of strands. He had his choice, but he selected the one closest to her ear. The one that trailed across her collar bone. "Good. Since I'm not that kind of guy." He slowly tucked the strands behind her ear and kept his fingers going all the way around her neck where they lightly stroked her nape.

Fueled by echoes of her goals and dreams—and they were really faint now—Sophie clamped her hand around his wrist. "*Not* that kind of girl." She struggled to pull his hand away from her neck, not because he fought her, but because he didn't.

He didn't step back, but he did smile. "Sorry, but it looks like I *am* that kind of guy." He wrapped his arm around her waist and slid her across the damp floor until she was pressed against him, wet swimsuit and all.

And then he lowered his mouth until it was an inch above hers and held.

Sophie's eyes had drifted shut in response to the inevitable. Except it wasn't so inevitable after all. Her eyes opened and she saw him watching her. "I'm not the begging kind of girl, either."

"We'll see about that," he murmured and lowered his mouth.

5

IT WAS SUPPOSED TO BE one kiss. Together, they'd fought the elements and emerged victorious. Their hearts pounded. Adrenaline heightened their emotions. Juices were flowing. Urges were urging. What could be more natural than a kiss celebrating life?

Nothing. Which was why one kiss easily melted into another, and then another, and so on, until it became one long kiss that showed no sign of ending. And Adrian was perfectly happy to hold a warm, wet Sophie in his arms and kiss her until they were both senseless. He'd been in trouble since those pink flip-flops had first stood in front of him.

Look what she'd done to him. He was supposed to be driving home to Tulsa but within minutes of meeting her, she'd been lying on top of him and he'd forgotten Tulsa existed. He barely remembered Oklahoma. She'd fed him steak and fruit and a little wine and he'd started thinking clearly again. She'd solved his advertising issues. And she'd done it all while maintaining a strictly professional, matter-of-fact demeanor that, perversely, had driven him insane with good old-fashioned lust. Or bad old-fashioned lust.

Lust made people reckless. Lust made people, Adrian in particular, grab the nearest female—that would be

Sophie—and kiss her in the way a man kisses a woman he intends to take to bed. Soon.

Luckily for him, Sophie was kissing him back with more enthusiasm than he'd expected from someone who'd insisted that she wasn't "that kind of girl." He didn't want "that kind of girl." He liked this kind of girl, especially the way she pressed her body against him. There wasn't much between them except some thin stretchy fabric and his shorts. Which was too much. Which he could remedy by unfastening her swimsuit at the neck and peeling it off her. She'd be much more comfortable without that wet suit on.

It was a brilliant idea. Sophie wasn't the only one who could think of brilliant ideas.

As though she read his mind, her arms wound around his neck giving him easier access to the suit's sliding fastener. Adrian stroked his way up her bare back and tangled his fingers in the wet seaweed that was her ruined ponytail, prompting a gasp that broke them apart.

Her eyes were huge and her chest heaved.

Was she shocked? Surprised? Frightened? She sure wasn't the picture of lust, old-fashioned or otherwise. And why should she be? This was their first kiss. A really long, really great kiss, but, jeez Louise, he'd been seconds away from stripping off her suit and pushing her up against the wall. Slowly, gently and very reluctantly, he lowered his arms. "I'm sorry," he whispered.

Sophie stilled. "For what?"

"For…"

Raising an eyebrow, she tugged at the elastic in her hair. "For?"

This was a test. Adrian hated these types of tests. There was no way to pass these types of tests because only women knew the right answers and they weren't sharing. "For pulling your hair. For hurting you."

"And?"

There was no "and." He wasn't going to pretend there was. "I'm sorry we're not kissing anymore. I'm not sorry I kissed you and I intend to kiss you again. Longer. Harder. And wearing fewer clothes."

"Oh, good." She shook her hair loose.

She'd said "good." Good was good, wasn't it? Adrian's head pounded with the effort to think about anything other than the male prime directive—mate with female.

He needed to get Sophie from dripping by the front door to naked in the bedroom. *He* needed to get from dripping by the front door to naked in the bedroom.

So he took off his navy chino shorts and kicked them out of his way. Reaching for Sophie, he saw her eyes widen as she stared at him.

Admiration or fear? When she didn't say anything, Adrian slid his hand down her arm and gently grasped her fingers. "Are you okay with this?"

"I am *beyond* okay with this."

"Because we don't—"

"Yes, we do." She drew his hand to her waist.

"Good." He should say something more. "Great." Something pretty. Women expected to be romanced. He needed a romantic thought and he needed one now. He stared at Sophie and willed romantic thoughts. He stared at her mouth. He'd had his tongue in her mouth. He'd sucked her tongue into his. And then she'd sucked his tongue into—

"Adrian?"

Say something. "You— I— You're…" He had no romantic thoughts. His basic, primal thoughts had crowded out the romantic thoughts. He swallowed and tried again. "You are so…" Forget romance. He'd go for the truth. "I want you so much, I can't think. I can barely breathe."

She grinned. "Thinking is overrated. Concentrate on breathing."

"In a minute." Holding his breath, he reached beneath

her hair and unhooked the clasp of her swimsuit. Sliding the straps apart, he slowly peeled the wet suit down her body.

As each sliver of skin was revealed, Adrian's heart pounded harder, until he felt light-headed with anticipation. He pulled the suit over her breasts and stopped.

They were natural. Round. Soft. Perfect. He wanted to tell her so. Mostly, he just wanted to touch them, to take them in his hands and feel their weight and their softness and run his thumbs over her nipples to see if they'd tighten even more.

Sophie held very still, her eyes glowing an intense blue in the candlelight. "Breathe," she whispered.

"Okay." He gulped air. "Thanks." Breathing was good.

The oxygen revived him and clarified his thinking. Why was he restraining himself when the suit was keeping him from holding a naked Sophie in his arms?

In one movement, he stripped it all the way to her feet. Sophie gasped. Slipping an arm behind her knees, Adrian picked her up, feeling her cold, damp body and smiling when he imagined warming it.

He waited while she kicked the suit off her feet and then strode across the tile into the bedroom.

It was dark in the bedroom. There were windows, but the shutters and the stormy night blocked any light.

He set her down by the bed. "Don't move."

Adrian quickly retrieved a fat candle from the dining table and a towel from the bathroom. He took several steps inside the bedroom before the circle of candlelight touched Sophie's skin.

She hadn't moved.

They stared at each other in the flickering light, with the rain lashing the shutters and the wind humming and whistling in the background. Her skin gleamed a golden pink above intriguing shadows. She stood so still Adrian could have been looking at a painting or a sculpture. But she was a flesh-and-blood female. More important, she was Sophie. And she was waiting. For him.

Naked.

"Remind me to breathe again," he said.

"BREATHE," SOPHIE TOLD HIM in a breathy voice because she was having the opposite problem—hyperventilation.

Omigosh, the god of sex was about to make love to her. Wasn't there already a god of sex? Eros somebody? Too bad. He'd been dethroned by Adrian, with his perfectly sculpted torso, and his muscled shoulders, and his strong arms, and his serious thighs. *Serious* thighs. The candle he held picked out every valley of muscle and skin, shading hollows and burnishing biceps. This is how she should have photographed him, but she wasn't about to call a timeout now because a timeout would give her a chance to think and Sophie didn't want to think. This was purely physical. A one-time indulgence due to the storm and Adrian was good to go. Yeah, he had the equipment; she hoped he knew how to use it.

He didn't say much, but his eyes told her he liked looking at her and liked what he saw. He focused entirely on her.

This man was in the body-sculpting business, but Sophie instinctively knew that he wasn't comparing her to anyone else. He appreciated her for who she was and how she looked right now.

Heady stuff. Exciting stuff. To be honest, it was the stuff of fantasies. And as long as Sophie kept treating this as a one-time fantasy, she should have a, well, fantastic time.

Setting the candle on the bedside table, Adrian wrapped Sophie in the towel and rubbed her skin, warming her, sensitizing her.

A smile tugged the edge of his mouth. "This is for you," he murmured. "All for you. I want to see you mindless with passion and know I'm responsible. I want you to trust that I won't lose control. Because I won't."

That didn't sound right. Oh, sure, parts of it sounded really fabulous, but as a whole, no. "What if I want you to lose control?" she asked.

"Sophie." He pressed his forehead to hers.

"What if *I* want to see *you* mindless with passion and know I'm responsible?"

"Then we'll need condoms."

"Did you look in the nightstand? Or in the bathroom?"

He exhaled softly. "I didn't bring any."

"Neither did I, but Jonathan stays here. He's no Boy Scout, but he's always prepared. Check the drawer."

She watched as Adrian tugged at the knob. The drawer was caught on something and when Adrian worked it open, they saw that the something was an unopened box of condoms. Next to it were dozens of individual packets, tubes and bottles of various oils and lubricants, and an energy bar. Not Adrian's brand, but Sophie figured that under the circumstances, Adrian would give Jonathan a pass.

"Can we get back to the mindless passion now?" she asked.

"Absolutely." Adrian drew the towel away and kissed her.

It was a knee-buckler of a kiss. Yes, already. This was going to be good. So, so good. They'd get rid of all the tension and awareness between them and wake up relaxed and ready to get back to work on Adrian's campaign. Sophie slipped her arms around Adrian's waist and let her hands wander all over the deliciously defined muscles of his gluteus maximus, as he would say. And there was the little hollow on either side that people in good shape developed. She loved those little hollows. Later, she'd get to stare at the hollows. Maybe while he slept. He'd be magnificent in sleep, with the sheet bunched artfully around him. Or not. And maybe they could go skinny dipping in the ocean at dawn. A naked Adrian standing in the ocean at sunrise—

"Hey. Where did you go?"

Go? *She* wasn't the one who'd stopped the kiss. She blinked up at him.

He cupped her neck and combed his fingers through her damp hair, smoothing it away from her face, over her shoulders. All the while, his gaze was fixed on her eyes, mesmerizing her, pulling her into a place he was creating for the two of them. He was connecting with her, Sophie thought. Connecting emotionally and mentally.

But not physically. She stood on tiptoe and pressed a kiss to his lips to remind him. She'd intended it to lead to something more but, while he didn't *not* kiss her back, he didn't pull her closer or lean down, which left her standing on tiptoe. Slowly, she lowered her heels, keeping her head tilted, feeling her lips leave his.

"Open your eyes."

He was breaking the mood. Irritated, she stared up at him and saw eyes dark with banked desire looking deep into hers. "I want you with me. And I want to be with you."

Uh-oh. He was telling her that he didn't want merely a physical joining, he wanted it all—body, mind and heart.

And he was waiting until Sophie unwrapped her emotions, put them out there and engaged herself one-hundred percent. Until she connected with the man inside the body.

She looked away. He wasn't just passing the time; he was making this real, darn it. And once the fantasy became reality, there would be no sheepishly blaming the storm and going back to Sophie, the P&D employee, and Adrian, the client. She'd either be Sophie, the client's girlfriend who slept her way into a Super Bowl campaign—assuming she'd even be allowed to work on it—or Sophie, who stupidly blew a huge opportunity and got her heart broken.

Adrian was the perfect fantasy man and these were the perfect fantasy circumstances. Why couldn't he leave it at that?

"Sophie." Just her name, said quietly as his thumb stroked her cheek, a slight smile telling her he knew she was holding back.

She groaned inwardly. Did he have to be so...so *fantastic?* Why did she have to choose between a fantastic man and a fantastic career opportunity? Because no matter how they felt about each other, Sophie knew how their relationship would be perceived. If she ultimately worked on his Super Bowl campaign, she'd forever have an asterisk beside her name in people's minds: Member of ad team, but sleeping with client at the time.

She didn't want a relationship. She wanted sex. And sex with Adrian would be great. Really, really great. Why couldn't they just tumble onto the bed and get on with it?

His thumb moved across her cheek making her think of Adrian first and the sex second. Making her think that with her heart on the line, the sex could be transcendent and how often did a person get the opportunity to have transcendent sex?

"I changed my mind. I don't want mindless passion," he murmured. "I want memorable, unforgettable, momentous passion. I want you. Here. With me, not lost in your head somewhere."

Darn it. There would be other career opportunities, but there wouldn't be another Adrian.

Okay. She was tired of holding back. She wasn't a holding-back kind of person. So, okay. She was all-in.

She deliberately relaxed, feeling tension, both mental and physical, leave her body. And then she gazed into Adrian's eyes.

They warmed as his smile curved. "There she is." And he kissed her.

The kiss sizzled all the way to her toes shocking every part of her into full awareness. It was one turbo-charged kiss, kicking things into turbo speed, turbo intensity and turbo sensation.

When Adrian's lips moved against hers, Sophie wasn't just aware of the movement; she noticed their texture, their warmth, and their firmness.

When Adrian's hands stroked her skin, she felt the contrast between the calluses on his palm and the smoothness of his fingers.

When she ran her hands over his back, she noticed both the taut satin of his skin and the cords of muscle rippling beneath it. His touch stirred longings deep within her. The more they touched, tasted and explored, the more she craved. The sensations were both too much and not enough.

A storm equal to the one outside strengthened within her. Within Adrian, too, she sensed. His hold tightened, his movements lost their finesse and she felt a tremor in his arms that excited her. She'd done this. She, Sophie, had made this man, this gorgeous, intense, driven, intelligent, thoughtful, honorable man tremble with desire.

She trembled, too. It was the integrity that did it. Well, and the gorgeous, smart part, too, but there were lots of smart, good-looking men who couldn't be trusted. Jonathan came to mind, but only briefly because Adrian dipped his head and ran his tongue over her nipple.

Moaning softly, Sophie tilted her head back and tunneled her fingers into his hair as Adrian's tongue made her forget everything but him. Every swirl of his tongue caused an increasing ache deep within her. She heard more moaning and wasn't sure if the moans came from her or the wind outside.

She was ready for him and slipped her hand between them, trying to touch him, but Adrian clutched her thighs and fit their bodies together, trapping her hand against his solid stomach.

Sophie whimpered in frustration.

Adrian kissed her forehead. Her *forehead.* She opened her eyes to find him staring at her.

"Still with me?" His voice was so rough, she barely made out the words.

"I'm *trying* to be!"

He kissed her temple. "It's the journey, not the destination."

"I can't believe you said that."

He kissed her cheek, butterfly soft.

She was going to scream. And not the good screaming, either.

He feathered a kiss on her jaw.

Sophie put a hand on either side of his face and raised it until she could look him directly in the eyes. "Adrian! I want the destination. We can sightsee later."

Pulling her hands away from his face, he kissed her palm, his tongue tracing a lazy circle that made her skin prickle. Raising his head, he gave her a scorching look. "Then let me drive."

"Okay," she said, because that was some look.

Drawing her arms over his shoulders, he bent his head. But instead of the long, slow kisses she expected, he planted quick, hard ones on her neck, her throat, her collarbone. Urging her backwards, he suddenly reversed their positions so that instead of Sophie falling on the bed, Adrian did, bringing her on top of him.

He grinned up at her in the candlelight. "Here we are again. If you want to wiggle around, please feel free."

She was going to wipe the grin off his face. Slowly, she rocked her hips from side to side, forward and back over his hard length. Then, arching her back, she skimmed her breasts against his chest.

His breath hissed between his teeth. He no longer grinned.

Driving, ha. She'd show him driving. Sophie continued to

rotate her hips as Adrian's jaw tightened. Dipping her head, she licked along his jaw to his ear lobe in one long swipe. Then she retreated, dragging her nipples over him as she did so.

And then she did it again, arching her back and grinding her pelvis against his.

Before she could move away, Adrian clamped his hands on either side of her hips to hold her closer. Sophie couldn't reach his mouth. Wiggling in earnest, she scooted up his chest until she could kiss him. He allowed her one deep kiss before flipping her over.

"Hey!" Anything else she would have said was forgotten as one of his hands slid from her thigh to her breast while the other parted her legs.

He began stroking her and the ache intensified to a degree she'd never felt before. *This must be the transcendent part,* she thought as she bucked against him and dug her fingers into his back. The house could have disintegrated around them and she wouldn't have known or cared. There was just Adrian and his mouth and his fingers and the warm, heavy weight teasing her thigh.

She shocked herself by biting his shoulder.

Adrian gasped and moments later pushed into her. He'd barely moved before Sophie sobbed her relief as waves of sensation rolled through her.

"Don't stop," she managed to gasp.

"I never want to stop." His voice was ragged in her ear. "I can't stop. You're it for me, Sophie."

His words squeezed her heart and the ripples of her earlier passion intensified. "You're going to make me fall in love with you."

She hadn't intended to say it aloud, hadn't known she'd said it aloud until Adrian raised his head and whispered, "Good."

The look on his face made her a little dizzy or it could

have been that the slowly increasing rhythm he set made her inhale too quickly until she held her breath as a climax rolled through her once again.

Adrian rocked against her, prolonging her pleasure until at last, he shuddered, breathing her name, and touched the deepest part of her, claiming a piece of her soul.

6

"YOU CAN DRIVE ANYTIME, anywhere." Sophie stretched contentedly. It was four-thirty in the afternoon and she was still in bed with Adrian.

The storm outside had passed and earlier, she and Adrian had raised the shutters which allowed them to open the windows and enjoy the gentle breezes. This was good since the power still hadn't been restored.

But Sophie didn't care. She and Adrian had been awake all night talking and making love. At one point, when the storm had lessened, they'd stood naked outside in the wind and rain, cooling off since the inside of the beach house had become hot and sticky.

Sophie barely recognized herself. Never had she indulged in such an orgy of pleasure, both receiving and giving.

She'd risked her deepest emotions and her reward was Adrian. Looking over at him, she discovered him watching her, his eyes lazy and knowing. She'd never been so attuned to a man before. Sighing, she knew she'd never settle for anything less, not that she was going to have the chance. Adrian was The One. Oh, sure, they'd only been together a day, but it had been a heck of a day. The same as weeks for other couples. Still, she wasn't going to do anything rash. They'd have to try out their relationship in the real world.

And *then* she might do something rash.

She propped herself on her elbow and faced him, idly tracing his sensational muscle definition with her fingers. Not as much fun as using her tongue, but they'd just awakened from a lovely nap.

Adrian closed his hand over hers. "That tickles."

"You like tickles."

"Yes. But right now, I'm hungry."

"Mmm. So am I."

He laughed. "For food. I need my strength."

"Good, because I'm starving."

Adrian laughed again as he stood and pulled on his shorts. The late-afternoon sunlight caressed his skin and Sophie exhaled on a sigh. She'd never tire of looking at him.

"Another thing—now that the weather has cleared, do you think the folks who were supposed to come last night might show up?" he asked.

His words were like being doused in ice water. "Omigosh, you're right!" Sophie leapt from the bed and searched for her underwear, last seen when they'd gone outside to work with the storm shutters. "I've just been so…" She slid a glance toward him in time to catch his self-satisfied smile. No need to finish her sentence. "But it would be awful if someone from Peck and Davilla caught us like this." She pulled a tank top over her head. "Or if Jonathan caught us like this. What a disaster!"

Sophie was pulling on her shorts when she noticed that Adrian had gone very quiet. "What?"

"It might be awkward or embarassing, but a disaster?"

"Well, not a disaster for you, but for me, it would—careerwise."

"Why?"

Did she have to spell it out? "Because if nobody knows

about us, if we keep our relationship quiet, I can still work on your campaign without people thinking it's because I'm sleeping with you."

"I see."

But he didn't sound convinced so she kept talking. "Getting credit for a Super Bowl spot in my portfolio, especially at my age, is huge. It'll make my career. Unless it bombs—and it won't—I'll get promoted for sure…my own accounts…probably my own team…and I don't want my achievement tainted." *Tainted* didn't sound so good, even though it was accurate.

More silence. Not the content, sated, lazy afterglow silence they'd experienced several times, but the not good silence.

"So you want to sneak around."

Tainted had definitely been the wrong word to use. "Adrian! I'm just saying we should keep it to ourselves for a few weeks. Honestly, it would be best for you, too. My ideas for refocusing the Lean Machine campaign are solid and I don't want Jonathan or Ross—he's Jonathan's number-two guy—I don't want them ignoring my input because of—" she made a little gesture "—us."

Sophie couldn't read his expression, maybe because he stood in front of the window and the late-afternoon sun was behind him. Whatever that face meant, she didn't like it.

"So if there's no Super Bowl ad to worry about, then we're okay."

Sophie froze. A chill literally passed through her. Moving very slowly, she snapped and zipped her shorts and slipped her feet into her flip-flops. "You changed your mind?"

Their positions had shifted slightly and Sophie could see his face better. She really, really, really hoped he wasn't testing her.

"No."

She knew there was more. "You don't want me to work on the campaign."

"I don't think you'll be able to."

"If you ask Jonathan to put me on the team, I will. Those are my ideas."

"I know, but Jonathan pitched the green campaign. The Lean Machine proposal you fixed came from Mod Media."

No way. Her chest felt tight. "Mod Media out of Dallas?"

Adrian nodded, watching her carefully.

"Another agency? You hadn't hired an agency yet? You were deciding between P&D and Mod Media?" Her voice rose a little. *Stay professional.* "I assumed both ideas were from P&D." Which he'd probably figured out and which would explain his earlier expression.

"There were other agencies, but I'd narrowed it down."

Forget being professional. Sophie threw up her arms. "And *that's* supposed to make me feel better? I've not only lost our agency a multi-million dollar account, I've tweaked the competition's proposal?"

"You said it was better."

"It is." She couldn't believe Jonathan. The green thing was totally Mod Media's style, but clearly, they'd listened to the client while Jonathan had tried to out-Mod Mod Media. "But I thought it was ours. Do you honestly think I would have spent hours working with you—giving you *really* great stuff to take to the competition?"

"I thought you believed in me and what I'm trying to do. I thought we'd made a real connection." His expression turned bitter. That one, she had no trouble reading. "But it was just about the campaign for you. Oh, yeah, and putting a Super Bowl ad in your portfolio which you've mentioned, oh, about ninety-five times."

She stared at him across the rumpled bed, the bed that

reeked of sex. She could not have this conversation here. Whirling around, Sophie blindly walked through the nearest door, which happened to be the bathroom. More to keep her emotions under control than anything else. She gathered her toothbrush and other toiletries and stuffed them into her cosmetic case.

"Sophie." Adrian stood in the doorway behind her, reflected in the mirror.

She'd finished gathering her things but she wasn't about to push past him. Grabbing her brush, she yanked it through her tangled hair which brought tears to her eyes. What a good cover in case she actually did break down. Which she would, but not here. Not now. Not in front of Adrian.

"Sophie, I'm sorry. I didn't mean that."

She met his eyes in the mirror. "Yes, you did." Jamming her brush in the case, she decided to risk pushing past him after all.

He moved aside. Sophie scanned the living room as she flip-flopped her way across the tile to her suitcase, which was still open on the floor beside the kitchen. She hadn't unpacked much. Tossing in the cosmetic bag, she continued through the kitchen to the laundry where she'd hung up their wet things. Her skirt and suit and cover up were still damp. Too bad. She grabbed them and headed back to her suitcase.

"Sophie."

Ignoring him, she dumped her wet stuff into her suitcase and zipped it.

"Sophie, stop. I want you to work on the campaign. Your ideas are the best part."

"I'm sure it won't be difficult for Mod Media to incorporate them." No one else ever had any trouble using her ideas.

"I won't go with Mod Media. You can tell Jonathan what to do and I'll give Peck and Davilla the business." He smiled crookedly and dropped his hands on her shoulders. "Can we kiss and make up now?"

Sophie blinked at him. What happened to being totally attuned to each other? "You think I'm angry because P&D will lose the account?"

"Aren't you?"

"I'm disappointed. It's typical in the business. You win, you lose, you move on. I'm angry because you knew, you *had* to have known, that I was unaware Mod Media was in the picture and you didn't tell me. I think you didn't tell me because you were afraid I wouldn't help you."

"Would you have?"

Actually, Sophie didn't resent the question. "I wouldn't have been able to stop myself. I love the creative process." She spread her hands. "It's the way I am. But I would have been more discreet in expressing my opinions and I sure would have worked with the P&D ideas so you'd go with us."

"Didn't you hear me? I *am* going with P&D. Congratulations."

It killed her, but Sophie shook her head. "Mod Media came up with the original concept. Go with them." Sophie turned away and dragged her suitcase to the door. Sometimes doing the right thing really sucked.

"Sure. And when I do, that's the end of us. Unless there was never supposed to be an 'us.'"

"Meaning?"

"Maybe you were just here to close the deal."

Unbelievable. And it hurt. Boy, did it hurt. Sophie walked across the room to the kitchen bar and grabbed her phone. Flipping it open, she punched in a number. "Jonathan? It's Sophie Callahan. Yeah, I'm at the beach house and it's fine. Listen, I'm here with Adrian Dean. I've had a chance to discuss the campaign with him and it looks as though he's going with Mod Media. The thing is, we really hit it off, and it would be too awkward for him to be working with one agency while I'm working for another. I mean, he'd always suspect me of spying for you or pressuring him to sign with P&D and I don't want that. So I'm resigning." She looked directly at a stunned Adrian. "I'll have a letter on your desk Monday."

Well, that certainly shut him up. His skin had actually paled. He should stick with the spray tan.

"I—I can't believe you did that."

"Oh, please. As if I would." Sophie snapped her phone shut. "Still no cell service."

His mouth worked. "So you didn't just quit?"

"Quit my job after one night with you?" She rolled her eyes. "The sex wasn't *that* great." She even sounded convincing.

"That's not what you said earlier."

"You hadn't just accused me of sleeping with you so you'd hire Peck and Davilla."

They stared at each other. This would be a good time for him to apologize.

"Sophie, you've got to admit how it looks."

It looked as though she'd just had a one-night stand, that's how it looked.

Cold fury. That's what she was feeling. An anger so intense it surpassed the explosive stage. "I'll admit that I don't like this conversation. I'll admit that you're pretty naive if you expect me to believe you thought Peck and Davilla gave you the use of a beach house that rents for $6,000 a week during high season without any expectations at all. You led us on."

He had the grace to look away.

"On the other hand, I told you to go with Mod Media. I told you they had the better campaign. But I can certainly see where you would assume I was practicing reverse psychology." She snapped her fingers. "Darn. My devious plan didn't work."

She slung her purse over her shoulder. She would have liked to have made a grand exit, but she needed her coffee grinder. Stalking into the kitchen, she yanked the cord from the useless outlet. The food could stay. She hoped it rotted.

"Sophie, you can't leave." Adrian stood in her path. "I've been outside. There's high water and debris all over the road. You'll have to dig out your tires."

"Then I'll dig out my tires." She slid open the door and dragged her suitcase outside.

Adrian followed her until she glared at him with an expression designed to wither at fifty paces.

"It's not safe," he said.

"Lesser of two evils."

"Sophie, don't be stupid."

She gave him a tight smile. "Too late."

7

"I AM A PROFESSIONAL."

"I *am* a professional."

"*I* am a professional."

"I am a *pro*— Screw it."

It was Monday morning, just after seven-thirty. A soggy Houston was still drying out after the storm and a soggy Sophie had vowed to quit crying over Adrian.

He hadn't called. It wasn't until Sunday afternoon that Sophie remembered that they'd never exchanged phone numbers. Bodily fluids, yes, phone numbers, no. He didn't know where she lived, either. Oh, sure, he could have called Jonathan…but she hadn't wanted to think about that. Until now. Now she was going to face Jonathan, find out what the heck happened to everybody on Friday night and give him a heads up about Adrian going with Mod Media.

Because she was a professional.

"He's not in today," Cammy told her as Sophie breezed by. "Ross is covering."

Not this, he wasn't. "I should speak directly to Jonathan."

Just then, the door next to Jonathan's office opened and Ross appeared, hanging on to the door jamb. "Cammy—can you find Sophie Callahan and ask her to see me when she gets in?"

Cammy pointed at her.

"Wow. You're good." He gestured for Sophie to follow him into his office.

And there sat Adrian Dean. It was only seven-thirty and already he'd said enough to make Ross look as though he'd bitten into a sour apple.

"Sophie, on Friday, Jonathan inadvertently broadcast a text that was clearly meant to be private."

"It wasn't clear to me."

"How could you possibly—"

"No harm done," Adrian broke in. "In fact it turned out to be lucky for me, because Sophie helped clarify my thoughts and it's entirely due to her that I've agreed to sign with Peck and Davilla." He gave her a tentative smile. He didn't do tentative well. It actually looked more like a grimace.

"And, uh, we'll see that you get some time with the team," Ross mumbled.

She gazed at him, expression unchanged.

"I want her *on* the team," Adrian clarified, proving he was no fool about *some* things.

"Sure, sure." Ross shifted in his seat. "Adrian told me your ideas. They're not bad."

"They're very good."

He shifted again. "On the surface, but when you've had more experience, you'll understand why they aren't the best for this client."

Sophie didn't bother to respond to Ross. Looking straight at Adrian, she said, "You let him talk you into the Green Machine, didn't you?"

"He felt the other campaign was stale."

"Have you signed anything yet?"

"No."

"Good."

"Sophie!"

She ignored Ross. "Go with Mod Media, Adrian. You don't owe me anything."

She heard the breath hiss between Ross's teeth. "Sophie—Adrian, will you excuse us?"

"No," Adrian said.

It made Sophie smile. "Ross, the whole Green Machine concept doesn't fit Adrian's goals for his company. Besides, it's stupid."

Ross dropped all pretense of affability. "You realize that after I talk with Jonathan, you'll no longer be working here?"

She realized. "Then who will you steal ideas from?"

"I never stole your ideas."

"True. You stole the credit."

"Sophie!" Adrian looked from her to Ross. "Don't fire her. I'll only sign if she'll be working on the campaign."

Ross sneered. "Oh, I get it."

"No, you don't." Sophie took Adrian's arm and even in the midst of all the drama, she flashed back to the feel of his skin and how she knew exactly the way it felt next to her naked body. "Come on. Ross, will you please tell Aire-An that she'll need to find a new partner?"

"Who?" he asked as Sophie led Adrian out of the office.

Adrian let her lead him to the elevators, but stopped her when she would have pushed the button. "Sophie. Your job."

Collateral damage. "It's time to move on. I think Jonathan was getting ready to put me on Ross's team and I'd never get credit for anything again. Leaving will be better for my career."

Adrian studied her for several moments. Without saying anything, he punched the button. The elevator opened almost immediately and they stood aside as workers boiled out. He and Sophie were the only ones going down.

"I don't have your phone number and I couldn't get a hold of anyone who knew you," he said as soon as the doors closed. "I ambushed Ross this morning."

Sophie watched the floor numbers at the top of the elevator instead of looking at Adrian. "I can't believe you were going to sign with P&D."

"I wasn't! At least I wasn't until you got yourself fired. I was counting on you to go off about the Green Campaign and then I'd tell Ross I needed time to think about it and then I'd follow you around until you'd speak to me."

She looked at him. "You were just playing Ross?"

"It's the only way I could get to you."

"Simple and effective. Not bad. Okay." Sophie crossed her arms. "So here I am. Now what?"

"Two issues. Two separate issues that are to be considered completely independent of each other. Number one, I do want you working on this campaign. I was going to have Mod Media contact you. I've got an appointment with them this afternoon. Since you're now conveniently available employment-wise, will you come with me?"

"To Dallas?"

"Yes."

"Okay."

"Now, I know what you're thinking…wait." He grinned. "You said okay? For real?"

Sophie nodded. "I'm unemployed. It's a job lead. But tell me what I'm thinking."

"That you don't need my help getting a job and you don't want Mod Media to hire you just because I make it a condition. And you really don't want people to think I made it a condition because we're sleeping together."

"Slept together. Past tense."

"That's the second issue." Adrian pressed the emergency stop, pushed her against the wall and then kissed her—long and hard and wearing way too many clothes.

Oh, she remembered this. Wanted this. He was in a really good negotiating position right now.

"I'm mad at myself for suspecting your motives," he said. "I'm sorry. I wasn't thinking clearly." He brushed her hair behind her ear. "You see, I hadn't been eating well and we asked an awful lot from one steak dinner."

Sounded reasonable to Sophie. Most anything he said at this point would. "So how are you thinking now?"

"Focused and crystal clear. I ate breakfast. Steak and eggs."

Just as she laughed, the elevator alarm went off. Adrian ignored it to kiss her again.

"Hey!" Sophie shoved at his shoulders and reached around him to start the elevator moving again. "Great thinking, but let's expand it."

His hands rested at her waist, keeping her close. "Okay. I want to see where this goes."

"You said Dallas."

"I mean us." He gazed down at her, focused on her and only her.

No sane woman could ignore a look like that from a man like Adrian. Sophie felt a thrill go through her and knew she was toast.

"What do you think?" He grazed his knuckles against her cheek. "Let me have another chance?"

"Come back to my place while I pack and you can convince me." She looped her arms around his neck. "I'm going to need a *lot* of convincing."

The elevator came to a stop and the door opened. Thus, the last time Sophie's coworkers saw her, she was being convincingly kissed by Adrian.

And no one was surprised to learn that she'd led the team that created the clever Super Bowl ads for Adrian Dean's Lean Machine.

Text Appeal

1

Ever since Mia Weiss had come to work at Peck and Davilla three years ago, she'd watched Jonathan Black go through women as if they were disposable coffee cups. Until recently, every woman at P&D had a Jonathan story—except Mia. Oh, sure, he flirted with her in about the same way James Bond flirted with Moneypenny. She worked in the P&D traffic department, which scheduled projects and allocated graphics and production resources, so Jonathan wanted to stay on her good side. But she didn't take his attention personally because he would have flirted with any woman in her position.

Not that she'd *wanted* to join the legion of Jonathan's Jilts, but it was difficult to remain confident of one's womanly attraction if Jonathan never asked you out. People assumed he had and when she was forced to admit that no, she and Jonathan had never dated, she had to endure their surprise, followed by a speculative look as they wondered what was wrong with her.

And she was his type! He went for young brunettes with hair hovering around shoulder-blade length, and Mia spent an extra thirty minutes every morning perfecting her thick, glossy, shoulder-blade-length hair.

Jonathan preferred a quietly sultry look with a worldliness that hinted at hidden passions. So Mia had thrown out a few hints, just to see what happened.

Nothing, that's what.

It was making her crazy. So a few weeks ago, on her thirtieth birthday, Mia had thought, *Screw Jonathan,* which she'd probably never do, and had cut her black hair quite short with little pixie bangs. She'd started wearing red lipstick and liquid eyeliner. Her new look cried out for black, elbow-length gloves, a cigarette holder and a martini.

It also gained her an extra half-hour of sleep in the morning.

Ironically, that's when Jonathan had finally asked her out. Mia accepted, figuring she'd enjoy a free dinner, a few laughs, end the evening with a smooch on the cheek, and she'd have her Jonathan story at last.

She had a great evening. Unexpectedly great. Apparently, so did Jonathan. He asked her out again and, to her surprise, she accepted again. When he asked her out a third time, Mia hesitated. She'd never planned to become involved with him. Sure, she was having a fabulous time—Jonathan was charming and charismatic—but he dated no woman exclusively for more than a couple seasons. Mia knew that; she reminded herself every time he gave her the special, toe-curling Jonathan smile.

But special, toe-curling Jonathan smiles would lead to special, toe-curling Jonathan sex. Soon, if he followed his usual timing.

Going out with him just to say she had was one thing, but Mia didn't want to be another notch on his bedpost, although he was an urban legend in that department, as well. She genuinely liked him and could truly fall in love with him. If she overlooked his failure to commit, he was about as perfect as a man could get.

And overlooking his failure to commit was where women went wrong with Jonathan.

So Mia vowed to play it cool, to break the pattern she'd seen over and over again. The key to dealing with Jonathan was to make him want her more than she wanted him. Commitment first, falling in love second. Her inspiration was Anne Boleyn's strategy with Henry VIII—preferably without the beheading.

She turned Jonathan down for a third date, and then held her breath. Women seldom refused Jonathan, and if they did, he rarely approached them again.

She was the only one not surprised when he gave her the rare second chance. Even then, Mia didn't sleep with him.

That had not gone over well.

She'd asked for time and exclusivity before she'd consider sleeping with him. At the end of the evening, she'd left him standing on her porch after kissing him on the cheek near his mouth, deliberately leaving a faint red imprint of her lips to give him something to think about.

That had been two weeks ago. Since then, Mia had looked as chicly glam and indifferent as she could while she waited to see if her gamble had paid off. But as the days passed without a word from Jonathan, she came to work each morning anticipating the arrival of the dreaded spa basket and the resulting walk of shame as she carried it to her car.

Now, instead of the basket, he'd sent the invitation to spend the weekend at the beach house. He was committing.

Mia exhaled. She'd kept her heart in the deep freeze to protect it from him. This weekend could be the beginning of a thaw. And if it wasn't, at least she'd have her own car if she needed to make a grand exit.

She looked down at her phone and made a face. He wanted her to bring steaks and breakfast because he might run late. Yes, she'd scheduled him for a time-consuming, first-client meeting on a Friday afternoon to poke at him a bit. Just a little reminder. And his crack about running late was in response.

Fine, she'd allow him that. She'd bring steaks. She'd bring the best steaks he'd ever had in his life. And it would be the best night he'd ever had in his life.

FOUR HOURS LATER, Mia decided it was the worst night in *her* life. It was inky black outside her car and raining so hard the headlights only illuminated the slanting raindrops about a foot in front of them. There were no streetlights, and she couldn't see the road. She couldn't see *anything.* And she was lost. Well, not really lost because Surfside wasn't that big, but she wasn't where she wanted to be. She'd been to the beach house once before, during the P&D Christmas at the Beach party, although she hadn't driven herself. She figured all she had to do was find the ocean and drive beside it until she came to a large, spectacular beach house. There weren't that many.

Except she couldn't see the ocean. How could she lose the Gulf of Mexico? She *thought* it was on her left, but she didn't recognize any landmarks, not that she could see them now anyway, and she wasn't entirely certain whether she was driving east or west.

The windshield wipers beat frantically but didn't do much good. Wind buffeted her Honda Civic causing her to grip the wheel until her hands cramped. The sprinkling of tiny lights from beach-house windows that she'd been using as a guide had gone dark maybe an hour ago. At this point, Mia wanted to find the main road back to the highway, pull into a parking lot somewhere and wait out the heavy part of the storm.

Earlier, with the rapidly worsening weather, she'd sent a text to Jonathan but hadn't heard back. Still in the meeting, she guessed. Now, she couldn't get a cell signal at all.

The car shook with the latest gust of wind and a large

piece of cardboard careened across the beam of the headlights, startling her. She jerked the steering wheel and felt a couple of bumps as the tires caught the edge of it, and reacted by yanking the wheel the other way.

Okay, stop. Just stop. Calm down.

Mia regrouped. Was she still on the road? The surface was nothing more than crushed oyster shell, so she couldn't tell by the way the tires felt.

Heart beating hard, she crept the car forward, leaning over the steering wheel and squinting into the darkness. She wanted to stop, but figured that keeping the car moving until she came to the nearest beach-house driveway and pulled in was the best strategy.

And it worked for about two minutes until a bulky shadow that looked like a mattress or a lounge-chair cushion loomed out of nowhere and *thwumped* against her car, pushing it sideways. Mia tried to compensate and the back tires skidded. And then, horrifyingly, the tires spun over nothingness and dropped, leaving the nose of the car pointed upward. Mia gingerly pressed the accelerator and felt the tires spin uselessly.

Unbelievable. She turned off the windshield wipers and listened to the rain beat against the car. Without the thumping of the wipers, the wind sounded ominously louder.

This could not be happening to her. She'd plotted and planned and acted with logic and deliberation. Jonathan was right where she wanted him—more or less. Probably less. And she was stuck in a ditch—actually, she didn't know that it was a ditch. But she did know that she was stuck, trapped in her car in a monster storm, alone, with no cell-phone signal.

Where had this stupid storm come from, anyway? The forecasters had said scattered showers and wind gusts. Was this meteorologist humor?

Mia turned off the engine and put on her emergency

flashers. If anyone else was driving in this mess, she didn't want them to run into her. And if, by some miracle she was actually on the road to the beach house, maybe Jonathan would drive by and rescue her.

Give it up, Mia. Jonathan was not going to be out driving to meet her in weather like this. He did like his creature comforts and he would have assumed that she had stayed home. No doubt there were messages from him in her voice mailbox. Which she couldn't access.

Mia leaned against the headrest. She'd been so smug about him coming around that she'd thought of nothing else but the next phase of her plan, the tricky part where she made him fall in love with her before she fell in love with him.

Playing a damsel in distress was not part of the plan. She didn't want to be rescued; she wanted to be wooed and won. And loved. Really and truly loved.

2

"KEVIN, WE'VE HAD A couple of calls about a stalled car around Leeward and Sun Fish, just off Beach Front Road. Are you in any position to check it out?"

Kevin Powell looked from the brisket he'd been slicing before he'd answered the phone, to the turkey breast, the mayo, the mustard and all the other sandwich fixings he'd laid out prior to assembling as many box meals as he could. He'd been half expecting a call like this one ever since the hurricane in Mexico had slid along a high-pressure system that squeezed the outer bands far more north than predicted. Now it sat churning in the Gulf and slapping the Texas coast.

Earlier, the Surfside police had driven through the beachfront neighborhoods and broadcast advisories, more to warn the tourists renting beach houses that the storm surge could flood their cars than the year-round residents who knew the drill. And, of course, to warn the novice surfers who were attracted by the waves and completely misjudged the undertow. Even so, there were always people who ignored the warnings and ended up needing rescue, thus endangering others' lives by their own stupidity.

Kevin had no patience for stupid people. "Sure," he told Charlie, who headed the volunteer emergency team. "I can drive over and see what's going on. But there had better be a pregnant woman in labor in that car at the very least. Anything less than a medical emergency and I'm liable to express opinions that will directly contradict all those friendly billboards the Chamber of Commerce put up."

He heard a weary chuckle. "Thanks, Kev. And save me some of that brisket, will you?"

It had already been a long day as surfers arrived and tourists left and beach-house owners secured their property against the coming storm. Great for his restaurant, Kevin's Patio, but exhausting. When the wind had picked up, he'd sent his two employees home and had tied down the patio furniture and umbrellas by himself.

After that, he'd monitored the police scanner as he packed potato salad and coleslaw into tiny foam cups. So far, the emergency personnel had everything under control, and it seemed the storm would be a big, wet nuisance more than anything else.

Once the power had gone out, Kevin had known he'd lose the contents of his coolers, so he began assembling box meals and prepared to take them to the public shelter in nearby Freeport.

And now a call had come in. Staring at the kitchen prep table, he shook off his weariness. He'd have to shove the perishables back into the cooler, which would let out precious cold air. The rescue better be worth it.

Kevin's truck was fit with a wheel lift and towing winch, mostly because people kept leaving their cars illegally parked and blocking access to his restaurant while they spent the day at the beach. Rather than bother the police, he moved the cars out of the way himself.

He also lent a hand when emergency services got strained. Like now.

Kevin tossed a first-aid kit in with the spotlights and blankets and drove out into the rain. The five-minute drive took twenty as he avoided debris and a high tide that covered the unpaved roads. It was slow going even with the spotlights augmenting the truck's headlights. Eventually, he saw the nose of a car poking out of a flooded drainage culvert. The driver had the good sense to leave on the flashers even though the back ones weren't visible.

Pulling a safety-orange rain poncho over his head, Kevin grabbed an industrial-strength flashlight and forced his door open against the wind.

Before approaching the car, he shined the powerful beam at the interior and saw a hand raised against the glare. He couldn't see anyone else in the car. Approaching, he kept the beam fixed on the driver. Once he got close enough to make out that the driver was female and was now shielding herself from the light with both hands, he tapped on the window and briefly turned the light on himself before directing it away from her face.

"Need some help?" he shouted at the still-closed window. It was probably electric and she'd turned off the car.

There was movement in the car. He waited, his shorts getting splattered with sandy water beneath the poncho. The window lowered about an inch.

"Need help?" he repeated. "We've had calls about your car."

"Can I see some ID?" he heard.

He blamed too many *CSI*s on TV for this. Yes, she was correct to ask, but he hated that people felt they had to. He dug for his wallet, which meant that side of him got soaked, and shoved his license against the window.

"I can't see it," she said.

Kevin adjusted the flashlight beam.

"But that doesn't tell me who you *are*."

"Lady, I don't know who you are, either."

Wet and tired as he was, Kevin had to smile when she held up her own driver's license. Mia Weiss, Houston address, age thirty. Old enough to know better. "I don't suppose you're pregnant and about to give birth?"

"No!" The look she gave him was filled with wariness.

So she didn't have a sense of humor. "Mia, let's get you out of the car and I'll see if I can drag it back onto the road." Driving it might be another story, but he kept that to himself.

Looking through the wet glass, he made out Mia returning the license to her purse. She was shaking her head. "I want to see your official ID," he heard.

"A Texas driver's license is as official as I've got."

"No badge?"

Like they couldn't be faked. "I'm not a police officer or with the fire department or any other official rescue team."

"Then, thanks, but I'll wait."

"I'm it! There won't be anybody else!" Briefly, Kevin rested his forehead against the roof of her car. Briefly, because she was from the big city and probably had pepper spray. "They're all busy and sent me. This isn't Houston and I'm not some predator who enjoys driving around in the rain looking for victims. We're a small town and you can't afford to be picky!"

"Go away!"

They had to shout to hear each other, which was good because Kevin felt like shouting. "I should! I should get in my truck and go back to making sandwiches instead of rescuing people stupid enough to drive in weather like this." He dropped the flashlight beam and started walking to his truck, expecting her to call out to him.

But no. That would be the action of a rational person and she wasn't rational.

Except she was, from her point of view, which was that of a lone woman stranded on a deserted road. In fairness, he couldn't blame her. She was doing exactly what police advised women to do to protect themselves.

Stomping back, he yelled, "Look—call 9-1-1 and they'll vouch for me!"

"I can't get a signal!" Her hand flew to her mouth.

Yeah, she shouldn't have admitted that. They stared at each other.

"No-o-o signal," Kevin said in an ominous voice. Shining the light so it illuminated his face from beneath, he continued. "All alone, trapped in a car on a dark and stormy night at the mercy of whoever drives by. Bwahahaha!"

She stared at him, mouth agape. Snapping it shut, she looked away, but not before he caught a smile. Or maybe it was a distortion caused by the water dripping down the window.

He tapped to get her attention and dangled his truck keys at her. "C'mon. I'll let you drive."

The window lowered another inch and she stuck her hand out. He dropped the keys into her palm and they disappeared inside the car. The window closed.

And nothing.

She did *not* just take his keys and leave him standing there in the wind and rain. As the seconds ticked by, Kevin regretted his impulsive "trust me" gesture.

Fortunately, the handle moved and the door opened a crack. Kevin pulled, helping her open the door as far as it would open. She handed him an overnight bag and a plastic grocery sack and then worked her way out, one long leg at a time.

Nice legs. Belatedly, Kevin thought to lift his poncho over her, but she was already soaked.

She slammed the door shut. He offered her a hand and she crossed the flashlight beam as she climbed out of the ditch.

Kevin inhaled sharply. She wore a white cotton dress and

she did do great things for wet cotton. Such great things that he turned the beam on her and stood watching her spotlit hips wiggle as she jogged toward his truck.

Remembering that she had the keys, he hurried across the road to catch up just as she yanked open the driver's door. He was headed around the front of the truck to the passenger side when she called to him.

"Wait! You're seriously going to let me drive?" she shouted.

"Yeah."

"After I drove into a ditch? Are you nuts?" She tossed him the keys as she ran around the truck and got in the other side.

Okay, then. He returned the keys to his pocket and shoved her bags across the seat before climbing in after them and slamming the door.

Even though the rain beat on the metal roof, he could hear her shallow breathing. "I thought you'd feel safer if you drove," he explained.

"Not necessarily. You could have a gun and hold it on me."

"Nah." He shoved the poncho hood off his head. "I'd use a knife."

"But you'd have to get close to use a knife. With a gun, you'd control from a distance."

She wouldn't sound so sure of herself if she knew he could see through her dress. He turned off the flashlight. "Thanks for the tip."

Just then, chatter sounded from the truck's radio as different rescue units reported their status. And then he heard, "Kev, you copy?"

Glad of the distraction, Kevin picked up the microphone. "Yeah, Charlie. The car's in the ditch and I've got the driver here in the truck. Mia Weece—"

"Weiss." She pronounced it like "wice."

"Mia Weiss," he corrected. Said that way, her name tickled a memory, but he couldn't place it. "Houston address. No injuries, but she's a little nervous—can you vouch for me?"

"Sure." There was silence and Kevin knew Charlie was laughing. "Ma'am?"

Kevin handed the microphone to Mia.

"Yes?" she answered.

"Are you with a good-looking guy who drives a white truck?"

She eyed him. "He drives a white truck."

Charlie didn't bother to let up on the mike transmit button as he laughed. And he expected Kevin to save him brisket after this? There was going to be a tuna-fish sandwich with Charlie's name on it. Or maybe cheese on stale bread.

"Is he wearing a Hawaiian shirt?" Charlie asked.

Clicking on the flashlight, Kevin raised the poncho and Mia ducked her head to look.

"Yes."

"That's Kevin. I know he's got a suspicious air about him and I apologize for that, but we had reports of a possible stalled car and asked him to come take a look. We hoped he'd behave himself."

"Thank you." Mia handed Kevin the microphone.

"He was being sarcastic," Kevin pointed out.

"It was also unnecessary and unprofessional."

Kevin slid the microphone into its clip. "Isn't that a little harsh?"

"No." She gazed steadily at him.

Water drops dripped from the pieces of her hair stuck to her face. She didn't have much hair. In fact, his was longer.

He followed one droplet as it slid from her dark eyebrow down her cheek where it paused by her vivid red mouth. Lipstick. He wasn't a fan.

She was pretty, but in an urban, high-maintenance way. Kevin wasn't a fan of that, either. "Charlie was only trying to lighten the mood and reassure you."

"I wouldn't have gotten in the car if I'd needed reassurance."

He pegged her as one of those single, independent types, a little on the snooty side. He avoided those types. "What made you decide to trust me? The keys?"

"No. It was when you threatened to go make sandwiches."

Kevin tried to follow her thinking, but it made no sense. He suspected she was out of practice. "Good to know. I'll work that into more rescues."

"This isn't a rescue!"

At her outrage—her irrational, illogical, misplaced outrage—Kevin raised his eyebrows. And don't even get him started on her ingratitude.

"Okay, it's a rescue," she capitulated. "Thanks." She offered him a quick, shy smile.

Amazing how one little smile could wipe away most of his irritation with her.

"No problem." Except it was. She was. And before the night was over, she'd become a bigger problem. He could see it coming, but there wasn't a darn thing he could do about it. Kind of like the storm beating down on them.

Mia sniffed and brushed at the hair on her forehead. "I'm on my way to the Peck and Davilla Media Management beach house. Do you know it?"

It figured. "Yeah. I've catered for them before."

"Is it far? Can you drive me there?"

"Not tonight." He started the engine and turned on the back spotlights. "Too much water and debris on the roads and they aren't in the best shape to begin with. We still haven't quite recovered from Hurricane Ike."

"But—" She broke off as he backed up the truck. "What are you doing?"

"I'm going to *try* to pull your car out of the ditch and drag it off the road," he told her. "I emphasize 'try' because I don't do this for a living and I don't have commercial equipment."

"I understand. You want to be released from liability."

"This has nothing to do with whether or not you might sue me." Kevin was generally pretty easygoing, but he had his limits. "I'm giving you the option to leave your car here, where it might take on water in the back, and call a towing service in the morning, or take a chance that I can get it out of the ditch now."

She blinked at him. "Go for it."

He jammed the truck into Park. As he pulled up the poncho hood he nodded over his shoulder. "There are blankets in the back."

"Do you need help? Should I hold the flashlight or something?"

She got points for offering. "I got it." His hand was on the door handle when he added, "But promise me you won't drive off or try to move the truck."

"I wouldn't do that!"

"Good, because I don't want to get pancaked between the vehicles." Shoving open the door, Kevin stepped out into the wind-driven rain.

Storms sure were noisy.

And he hated the swirling wind. He'd rather have it all coming at him from the same direction instead of getting smacked around before he could prepare himself.

Kind of like women, now that he thought about it. Men were consistent and straightforward, putting everything they had into a focused offense. Women danced around and took pokes all over the place, smiling little smiles and keeping their opponent off balance.

And speaking of being off balance, getting her car back onto the road was going to be a good trick. Water eddied around Kevin's ankles and rain kept getting in his eyes as he prepared the winch.

In the process of trying to attach the tow hook to the chassis, Kevin had to climb into the truck bed and raise his arms. The poncho flapped into his face and rain doused his shirt and shorts. He might as well not be wearing any rain gear at all.

He finally got the winch hook attached to some piece of metal that looked as if it would hold, and jumped down.

Back in the truck he set the winch and slowly pulled forward, hoping he had the right angle to get her car out without doing something stupid like flipping it over.

"Can you watch out back and tell me when the car is clear of the ditch?" he asked her.

She twisted around. "It's hard to see."

Well, yeah.

Before he could stop her, Mia threw off the blanket and opened the door to jump out onto the road.

He really wished she hadn't done that. Through the windshield, he could see her waving him forward, she and that damn transparent dress clearly illuminated in his headlights. She had a pretty good shape from what he could see, which was a lot. The wind and the rain molded the dress to her body. Even what there was of her underwear was see-through.

Kevin's mouth went dry, in contrast to the rest of him. Forget the car. Forget the rain. Forget the fact that he didn't know her. He wanted to shove open the door, run his hands all over her, then lay her on the truck hood and bury himself between those long legs. Instead, he drove the truck forward until she motioned him to stop and got back inside.

"I appreciate the help," he shouted over the storm's roar. More for self-preservation than anything else, he draped the blanket across her shoulders and breathed easier when she closed the ends across her chest. Getting all worked up over her wasn't going to do any good.

After some more maneuvering and another trip into the rain, Kevin had her car on the opposite side of the road and parked in somebody's front yard, or what would be somebody's front yard if the tide weren't covering it.

"Thanks!" Mia said brightly enough to instantly rouse his suspicions. "I'll just—"

He grabbed her wrist.

"Hey!" She tugged and he held on.

"Stay in the truck." Kevin spoke with every ounce of authority he could muster. "You do not know if the car is drivable and even if it is, I am not going to let you drive it." He pressed the accelerator, putting as much distance as possible between her car and his truck as fast as he dared. He really wished he had the use of both hands.

"Let go."

"You'll jump out."

"What do you care?"

"Paperwork."

"Such compassion."

"You haven't seen the paperwork."

Mia responded by yanking her wrist and since Kevin held on, the truck swerved and skidded.

"Don't do that! You may have a death wish, but I don't!"

After several moments she asked in a cowed voice, "Where are you taking me?"

He hated that she sounded all beaten down. "My place—it's a restaurant. I'm going to force you to make sandwiches."

"Just how many sandwiches will it take to adequately express my gratitude?"

Was that a smile he heard in her voice? He glanced at her. "Until I run out of meat."

She raised an eyebrow.

"Brisket," he clarified. "Turkey. Maybe a little tuna salad."

Mia wiggled her wrist. "Oh, let go. Of course I'm staying in the truck."

Kevin released her in time to jerk the wheel to avoid somebody's lawn chair blowing across the road. "All this time and I had no idea invoking the mighty sandwich would be so effective."

Mia laughed unexpectedly and, for no reason at all, Kevin forgave her for inconveniencing him on such a filthy night. Her throaty laugh tugged at places inside him that had no business being tugged.

Her see-through dress might have had something to do with it, too.

There wasn't much talking as they made their way back to Kevin's Patio, which was good because he needed to concentrate on driving. Once inside the kitchen, he flipped on the back-up lighting and Mia tossed her wet blanket aside.

Kevin busied himself with wiping off the flashlight, hanging up the poncho, hosing the sand from his legs—all things that kept him from looking at her.

"My apartment is up the stairs. Take one of the lanterns. You can rinse off and change into dry clothes. If you want to, you can grab a shirt from my closet. Help yourself to whatever you need."

"Thank you."

He saw the glow when she turned on the lantern, but then it didn't move because she stood there. She stood there instead of going up the stairs. Why was she standing there? Kevin risked looking at her. He aimed his gaze to where he expected her eyes to be, but he'd always had good peripheral vision. The fluorescent lantern illuminated her entire body, which, thanks to the wet dress stuck to her, he could see perfectly. If she'd been the type to wear days-of-the-week underwear—and he saw she wasn't—he'd be able to tell today was Friday.

She had a *great* body.

Damn that peripheral vision.

He was running out of stuff to do. He needed to clean up himself before he began working with food.

Kevin didn't notice right away that Mia wasn't staring at him, but over his shoulder at a poster.

He knew the poster. The Chamber of Commerce had launched a tourism campaign and he'd allowed himself to be talked into modeling for it. It had saved them money and got him some free advertising.

There were other posters in the patio area, but this one, his Cowboy Surfer poster, Kevin had hung in the kitchen. To be honest, there were a couple more he wasn't hanging anywhere, ones he and the photographer had taken after the official shoot. The moon that night had been full and the sky clear and he and the female photographer had shared a bottle of wine and… Not that he was ashamed, but those photos were a little arty for the family crowd.

"I know you," Mia said.

It was funny how people saw your picture on a billboard and thought they knew you. "You've just seen my picture."

"No—I mean yes, but I work at Peck and Davilla. We did those ads. I'm Mia in the scheduling department. We've actually spoken on the phone a few times."

That explained why her name sounded familiar. "You're the one who set up the appointments with the photographer."

"Yes!" She smiled.

Kevin smiled back, but he was thinking that there was no way he would have connected the crisp, professional voice with the sexy, thong-wearing woman standing in his kitchen.

He was staring.

She was staring.

There was too much staring going on. Kevin gestured to the stairs. "You can go first. I've gotta…do stuff."

"Oh, sure. I'm sorry." Mia bent over to pick up her bag, outlining her hips, which showed pinkly through the dress, and were topped by a white lace T that disappeared between them.

Desire pooled in his groin and he just went with it, indulging his baser instincts, the ones that had her stripping off her clothes and him laying her out on the prep table.

Mia straightened and Kevin stared at the prep table, mentally rearranging the condiments. As she climbed the stairs he stole one last, lingering look.

Damn.

3

WAIT UNTIL SHE TOLD everybody at work that she'd been rescued by Kevin Powell, the Cowboy Surfer.

He'd been everybody's computer wallpaper last summer, specifically that poster—the one at sunset, where he and his perfect torso gazed into the gold-streaked ocean—which made Surfside appear better than it did in real life.

Kevin, Mia would happily inform her coworkers, looked just as good in real life. She suspected. She'd have to make sure when he wasn't wearing a wet Hawaiian shirt with his hair slicked to his head. And the fluorescent lighting wasn't nearly as appealing as the bronzy glow in the poster, so he should probably stand outside before she decided for certain.

Oh, and maybe he should wear those mirrored sunglasses that reflected the ocean as he had in the poster. And the straw cowboy hat. And the low-sung jean shorts. Without the shirt.

Especially without the shirt. Mia melted a little inside.

And especially with those frayed, worn, loose-fitting shorts that hung on his hips just, and she meant *just,* avoiding indecency. Not that a man who looked like that could ever be indecent. Kevin's image in her mind made her melt a little more.

*Any*way, now that she'd met him, he seemed like a genuinely good guy which made him even more attractive.

Unfortunately, his first impression of her wasn't so good.

During the drive back to Kevin's restaurant, Mia had become aware that she owed him more than the brief thanks she'd given him. Walking into his restaurant kitchen had brought home to her that he was a regular person who'd dropped everything to do her a favor at a whole lot of inconvenience to himself.

She'd been so focused on getting to the beach house that she hadn't realized she was in danger. It had all been so surreal. How many times had she watched the Houston news on TV and been disgusted by the people who drove their cars into standing water as though laws of nature didn't apply to them? Or watched rescues of people who ignored evacuation orders and marveled at their lack of common sense? She'd acted just like them.

Maybe the storm surge would have flooded her car, and maybe it wouldn't have, but she was lucky Kevin had refused to abandon her when she'd acted like such an idiot.

While she couldn't beat herself up over asking for ID, she could have been nicer about it. In contrast, he'd just sent her upstairs to his *home* without a thought.

He didn't know her. She could be a thief or a horrible snoop. Mia walked through the apartment living area into his bedroom. The closet door stood open and she couldn't help looking inside. Well, he *had* offered her his shirts. *The shirt off his back.*

Handsome, brave, strong, generous, responsible and a business owner. Probably thrifty, clean and reverent, too.

So what was the catch? Where was the girlfriend?

The bedroom was a bachelor's bedroom. Mia studied

the colorful row of Hawaiian shirts hanging in his closet. They were obviously his daily uniform and she suspected some were vintage collectables. He was supporting his brand identity—she worked in advertising; she understood. A straw cowboy hat sat on the shelf above the shirts. *The* straw cowboy hat, if she wasn't mistaken. She thought of the poster again and sighed a little.

No women's clothes. No chick pictures.

Another man who wouldn't commit?

Not her problem, was it?

Mia unzipped her bag and withdrew a white sleeveless top that tied at the waist, and some Bermuda shorts. Her sandals were wet, so she put on the plastic ones she'd brought to wear in the sand. Speaking of sand, she was splattered with dirty grit, so she went into the bathroom to rinse off her legs and arms before changing into dry clothes. Closing the door, she faced a full-length mirror.

And gasped.

Her white skimmer dress, which she'd thought looked so crisp and coolly sophisticated, was totally see-through. And not just a little bit. Spotlit by the lantern, she could see the lace design of her bra—also sheer, but it was sheer when it was dry, too. Wet, it was invisible. She could see her nipples, two dark circles in a sea of white. To be embarrassingly honest, it was difficult to look at anything else *but* her nipples. And she'd seen them before.

And now, so had Kevin.

Oh, and there was more. Mia forced her gaze southward. Yes, the matching lace thong, which was also sheer, and now revealed the skill of her waxing aesthetician.

As Mia stared, trying to convince herself that maybe her dress hadn't clung quite so much and that it had been dark outside so maybe Kevin hadn't noticed, she remembered him carefully avoiding looking at her in the kitchen. She remembered standing there holding the lantern just the way she was now.

She flushed—a whole-body flush that started in her upper chest and spread to her throat and stomach.

She knew because she could see it through her dress.

She'd stood in the light from the headlights, rain plastering her transparent dress to her body, and directed him as he pulled her car out of the ditch. She was lucky she still had a car.

Unless she didn't do it for him. How humiliating that would be. Not that she wanted him hitting on her, but when she'd spent weeks ogling his picture, she wanted to believe he'd at least felt a glimmer of interest when he'd seen *her* body.

Mia stripped off the dress and underwear, such as it was, and quickly rinsed off in the shower. She wished she had something other than a white top and more sexy underwear to change into, but she'd been going with a theme.

Mia hung her wet clothes over the shower rod and moved her bag out of the way. In doing so, she noticed posters propped against the wall by the bed.

Did he have an extra one of the Cowboy Surfer? After this was all over, maybe he'd autograph it and she could take it back to the office.

Mia set the light on the dresser and quickly flipped through the cardboard sleeves protecting the posters, stopping when she found some smaller, matted photographs. Pulling them out, she flipped the first one over.

And her jaw slackened. Nudes. It was the Cowboy Surfer without the jeans. Some in color, some in black and white and all exquisitely retouched and matted.

Most of the pictures were taken in moonlight, glorious studies of the male form in light and shadow. Glorious studies of *Kevin's* form. And it was a very fine form. Mia traced the line of his thigh and the curve of his buttocks. She could almost feel his skin beneath her finger. She *needed* to feel his skin beneath her finger.

Forget the Cowboy Surfer. Give her extras of these, especially the one of him looking across his shoulder directly at the camera. As though looking directly at *her*. She wanted to lose herself in that picture. She wanted to put it on her bedroom wall and talk to it every night. If the Chamber of Commerce had used this image for the tourism campaign, hordes of women would have immediately headed to Surfside.

Reluctantly, Mia put the pictures back and leaned the posters against the wall the way she'd found them. Then she went back downstairs where she tried to act nonchalant.

She found Kevin grabbing food from a large refrigerator and piling it on the stainless table as fast as he could. He glanced at her without breaking his rhythm.

In just that brief moment, his eyes swept over her, and she had no doubt that he was comparing her appearance now with the wet-T-shirt-contest-winning outfit she'd worn earlier.

So much for nonchalance. Her face and throat grew hot. She knew he was thinking of her naked, so she thought of him naked, which didn't help, but was very enjoyable.

Closing the door to the fridge, Kevin cleared his throat. "If you'll unwrap this stuff, I'll get cleaned up. There are aprons on the hook in the closet."

Mia immediately opened the closet door so she'd have an excuse to turn away from him as he walked by her. She faced the closet until she heard him reach the top of the stairs.

Closing her eyes, she exhaled. She was going to have to get over herself. In addition to his other sterling qualities, Kevin was clearly a gentleman. She'd carry on as though nothing had happened.

All right then. Aprons. They were bibbed style in either khaki or a sea green with "Kevin's Patio" printed on them in golden orange. She chose sea green since khaki wasn't one of her colors. Not that it mattered.

As Mia tied the apron behind her back she assessed the workspace, and then arranged the sandwich materials into the most efficient order. After that, she folded the carryout boxes so they'd be ready for the sandwiches, and positioned the plastic-utensil and condiment packs next to the boxes.

She wasn't sure how Kevin wanted everything put together, but noticed that the brisket was only partially sliced. She eyed the thickness of the slices and was cutting the rest to match when Kevin came back down the stairs.

He looked the same only dry. However, Mia knew exactly what was hiding beneath the loose-fitting Hawaiian shirt and baggy shorts.

"Hey, good work." Hands on hips, he surveyed the kitchen. "But I should have told you to use plastic gloves."

"Oh, it never occurred to me. Can we still use the meat? I did wash my hands. I know enough to do that."

He held out a box of plastic gloves. "Under other circumstances, it might be a health-code violation, but since I'm donating this stuff, it'll be okay."

Donating. Why didn't he just put on the halo and be done with it?

"Now, if any of the meat dropped on the floor, that's another thing. There's no three-second rule. Lorrie from the animal shelter comes by for scraps."

Mia slipped on the gloves. "And I'll bet there's always enough meat to justify her trip, right?"

"We can get a little clumsy." Smiling, he regarded her setup on the table. "What's going on here?"

"I figured we'd have an assembly line. One person does bread, one person does fillings. Then we bag and box."

"Huh." He studied it a few more moments. "I never thought about setting up like this."

"It's what I do," Mia said. "I identify the scope of the job, estimate how much time it will take, and then figure out the most efficient and cost-effective way of accomplishing the task with the available resources." *Relax. Don't lecture.*

"Okay, then." He glanced up, barely made eye contact and gestured to the bread. "You do bread and I'll do meat."

"Both mustard and mayo? Some with just one?"

"Barbeque sauce goes on the brisket sandwiches. Nuts. I forgot to get it out. At this rate, I'm not going to have any cold air left." Still without looking her way, he opened the fridge and brought out a container and set it near her. "And make sure you spread all the way to the edges. People complain if you don't."

"Really."

"Yeah." He cut up the rest of the brisket.

"So I guess we're doing brisket first." Mia split open the buns and slathered them with sauce. When she finished, she walked behind Kevin to get the onions and pickles. "Does anything else go in the sandwiches?"

"No. And only put onions in half of them. We'll mark the boxes." He worked quickly, but so did she.

"Let me show you how to wrap them," he said.

Setting the sandwich in the middle of a square of white paper that was shiny on one side, he folded the corners in. "Got it?"

"Yes." It wasn't rocket science.

Mia folded one sandwich. Midway through the second one she stopped. They were being so carefully polite. And the stilted conversation and the no eye contact was killing her.

"What?" Kevin asked.

"Look at me."

He did briefly and immediately went back to wrapping sandwiches. "Something wrong?"

"Yes! You've seen me naked. Or close enough."

That got his attention.

"I saw myself in the mirror, so I know. And it's making everything weird with me wondering if my dress was really that transparent and you—"

"Yes."

She drew a breath. "And you were wondering if I knew. So I know. Now." She exhaled. "Sorry about that."

"There's no need to apologize."

And right there, with that little sliver of a grin, she knew Kevin had liked what he'd seen, which pleased her way more than it should. "There might be. I saw the posters in your room. And the pictures."

He said nothing.

"The matted ones. Of you. Naked. At the—"

"I know the ones." He studiously worked with the sandwiches.

Was he embarrassed? "The pictures are great," she told him. "They're really beautiful, which is a strange thing to say about a man, but they truly are. You're very…"

He'd turned his head to look at her with exactly the same angle and expression as in the photo upstairs. Picture Kevin, who made her insides quiver, merged with Real Kevin, who made her want to push the food off the table while he ripped off his clothes. And then ripped off her clothes.

Not a good idea to let him know that. "So what I'm saying is that we've both seen each other naked or the next best thing—"

"There is no next best thing to naked." He gazed steadily at her, lips curved in the barest of smiles while his hands wrapped white paper around the sandwiches. "Want me to prove it?"

Oh, yes. Yes, please. She flashed to the matted pictures and got goosebumps. All that smooth, taut skin pressed against her body… She focused on the man standing about a foot away from her and got goosebumps on goosebumps. "No." Liar. "I believe you." Oh, so very true.

"You sure?"

Regrettably. "Uh-huh."

"Okay, then."

Blindly, Mia stared at the sandwich in front of her and finished wrapping it. She'd been worried about Kevin not making eye contact out of awkwardness. But after that sizzler, it occured to her that a little eye contact went a long way. "Um, I'll start putting mustard on the white bread." *And keep my eyes to myself.*

They worked in silence for a couple of minutes before Kevin asked, "What's going on at the beach house this weekend?"

"Nothing. I was supposed to meet Jonathan Black there. It was a spur-of-the-moment thing."

The whole atmosphere in the kitchen changed. "Oh, you're one of those."

Mia didn't pretend to misunderstand. She stopped spreading mustard on the bread and turned toward him. "I am not 'one of those.' I have gone out of my way not to be 'one of those.'"

"It's none of my business." Kevin carried the turkey breast over to the automatic slicer and fit it against the blades.

"No, it's not. But I don't want you getting the wrong idea."

Kevin pushed the turkey against the blades and thin slices of turkey fell into a pan. "Why do you care what I think?"

"Because..." Without considering, she blurted out the truth. "Because you seem to be a great guy and I couldn't stand it if you thought I was just another of Jonathan's disposable women." She was surprised at how much Kevin's opinion mattered.

"How are you different from the others?" He carried the turkey back to the table. "Because you're *in love?*"

"No, I'm not in love with him! That would be stupid."

Kevin raised his eyebrows. "Are you saying this was

supposed to be a business meeting or that you're just friends? Because you sure weren't wearing platonic underwear."

Mia took a moment to get past the underwear jab. "I told Jonathan I wouldn't get involved with him unless he was serious and willing to give our relationship a chance to develop. I asked for time and exclusivity. Then, if it doesn't work out, we'll go our separate ways. Inviting me here shows that he's serious."

"So you're exclusive for the weekend and afterwards, he brings you here for my Sunday Brunch on the Beach, where he orders freshly squeezed orange juice, black coffee, a huevo-ranchero omelet made with two yolks and three whites and a whole-wheat-flour tortilla. I won't need to memorize your order because you'll never be back. Jonathan will, how did you put it? Decide it's not working out and you'll go your separate ways."

Mia blinked.

"Except for the short hair, you're just like the others."

"I…I'm not." She felt a little sick. "Anyway, I'm not falling in love with him until he's in love with me."

Kevin reached across her for more bread. She'd gotten behind with the mustard and mayo. "My guess is that you've never been in love."

"I have, but why do you think I haven't?"

"Because you think you can turn love off and on like a switch."

"I do not!" She set down the mustard jar. "But I do think a person can be smart about love. Avoid the people you shouldn't fall in love with and hang around the people you should."

Kevin gave a crack of laughter. "You don't believe that love can just suddenly appear and whomp you upside the head?"

"Maybe."

"'Cause that's what happened to me. One minute I'm

minding my own business at Texas Tech and the next…pow. There she was."

"She hit you?"

Kevin chuckled and pointed to the mayonnaise. Mia started slathering it on the bread. "We were crazy in love, but she was from Colorado and I was from here. First we tried it her way and lived in Colorado, but I hated the cold and the snow and the thin air. That's not real air in Colorado." He inhaled the warm, humid, salty air in the kitchen. "Now this is air. When you breathe this, you know you're breathing."

"Or possibly smothering underneath a wet blanket. So you were married?" she asked in a casual I'm-just-making-conversation way.

He nodded. "We tried living here for a time, too. And she hated it as much as I hated Colorado."

"You split up?" She'd stopped spreading again and he gestured for her to hurry up.

"Yeah. We were fighting all the time. My one regret is that we let it go on too long. Put us both off relationships for a time."

"Do you still love her?" Mia looked at him as she asked so she could see his face.

"Do I still love her?" He looked off into the distance. "I hate her less. I guess you could say that the man I was back then still loves the woman she was at the beginning. But time and a whole lot of drama brought out the worst in us. So no. We're done."

Mia stepped around him and started wrapping the turkey sandwiches. "But I'll bet that the next time love 'whomps you upside the head' you'll make sure you both can live in the same place before you get involved."

"Well, sure."

"Which is my point. You'll be smarter about love."

"Ha." He glanced at her. "I see what you're saying, but

I don't know if I agree. Now you..." He tilted his head and studied her. "I think you've been burned."

"More like scorched. I sat out a semester of college to follow my idealistic boyfriend to Paraguay. We lived with local families—not the same ones—and volunteered building a school."

"Good for you."

"Don't give me any credit." Mia shook her head. "I only did it to be with him. He made it sound so romantic and noble. But I barely knew any Spanish and my carpentry skills are even worse. And the boyfriend turned out to be really great with the concepts but not so much with the practicalities."

"Was he a whiner?"

"He was oblivious." Mia rolled her eyes. "Way too much 'our cause is worthy so our needs will be met' attitude. I hated being there and after three weeks, I hated him. But I stuck it out and when we left, there was a bright, shiny new school that the villagers were living in because it was so much better than their homes."

Kevin started laughing. "It's not funny, but that's so typical."

Mia laughed, too. "Even worse, he never got it. He never figured out that food and supplies hadn't magically appeared."

Kevin grinned at her. "What did you do? 'Cause I know you did something."

"Bartered building materials for a twice-weekly food delivery."

"I would have done the same thing."

"You wouldn't have had to. I can tell you're the type who would have checked on the details before signing up."

"True."

Ready to change the subject, she gestured to the pile of

sandwiches. "We should package these and get them out of the way."

"You're right. They need to be in the ice chest. Come on over here and I'll show you how to box them up. I've got potato salad and coleslaw to go with them." He lifted the lid on a large rolling cooler and showed her the little foam cups.

"Since you know exactly how you want the boxes packed, you do that and I'll close them up and mark the contents. We can work faster that way."

"Sounds like a plan." He flashed her a smile.

It was a nothing smile, a throwaway.

But it warmed her in a way that Jonathan's smile never had. And probably never would.

4

"HEY, CHARLIE." KEVIN rolled an ice chest into the shelter in Freeport, Surfside's slightly larger neighbor to the north. "You've got customers, I see." Kevin indicated the cots and a few families milling around.

"Mostly tourists from rentals." Charlie nodded toward the chest. "Got any brisket in there?"

"For you, I've got a moldy cheese sandwich."

Charlie laughed as Mia rolled a catering cart toward them. When he saw her, Charlie immediately perked up, straightening his posture and, if Kevin wasn't mistaken, sucking in his gut.

As for Kevin, he almost *almost* could look at her without thinking of her in that wet white dress, the one that outlined a body he'd be dreaming about for weeks.

"Who's this?"

"That's the stray I picked up."

Mia heard him and held out her hand. "I'm Mia Weiss."

"Charlie. I vouched for him." Charlie jerked his thumb toward Kevin. "Glad to see you're okay."

"I know. It was stupid to be out driving. I've been trying to make up for it." She pulled the cart against the wall and surveyed the people trying to get settled.

Charlie raised his eyebrows at Kevin.

Charlie had a tendency to matchmake. Kevin gave him a warning look. Not that he wouldn't mind hooking up with Mia, but they'd both gone the wrong way down the Road of Love before and neither was looking for a detour to nowhere.

"She helped me pack the food," he told Charlie.

"Then it'll probably be done right this time."

Mia heard and smiled at Charlie. She wore a white top and shorts and plastic-jelly sandals, but they looked dressier on her than on anybody else in the room. Kevin couldn't figure out how she did that, but anyone seeing her would know she didn't live around here.

"You want to see something done right then stick around," he said to Charlie. "Mia, I'm going to introduce you to Susan." Kevin raised his arm to attract the attention of a woman with her gray-streaked hair in a short ponytail.

She breezed over. "Thanks for the food, Kevin. The volunteers always appreciate it."

"It would only go to waste otherwise. I've got someone I want you to meet." He drew Mia over to them, lightly touching the small of her back.

That top she wore was just shy of the waistband of her shorts and his fingers grazed bare flesh. He hadn't planned anything more than a polite gesture, but heat and awareness zapped up his arm.

No. Not her. Please not her.

He knew what it meant. It meant he was attracted to her in a way that went far beyond a general appreciation of a good-looking woman. He'd been afraid of this ever since she'd helped him pack meals and had turned out not to be totally useless.

He gritted his teeth and plowed through an inelegant introduction. "Susan, this is Mia. She organizes. Mia, Susan runs emergency services and strong-arms people into giving her stuff."

"Kevin!" Susan protested.

Mia laughed. "He means you acquire resources."

"That sounds better."

Charlie snorted. "It may sound better, but people don't say no to Susan very often."

"They don't often say no to me, either," Mia said. "Susan, I was looking at the cots...do you mind if I rearrange them?"

"Not at all." Susan exhaled a tired sigh. "People have had to set up their own. We didn't have the chance to prepare the way we usually do."

"I know," Mia agreed. "It's like the storm came out of nowhere. Hey, while I've got you here, what about the food tables? How many are there and do you know where you want them placed? Because I have an idea."

"Please lay out things however you want." The two women started walking toward the cot area, still talking, with Mia gesturing and Susan nodding and making notes on her ever-present clipboard.

Kevin chuckled softly. "Charlie, brace yourself. The two of them are going to be a force of nature that will rival anything going on outside."

"Is that so?" Charlie asked.

"Oh, yeah."

After a moment Charlie said, "She's a good-looking woman."

Understatement. Kevin exhaled.

"You know, I think she might have been giving you the eye." Charlie was goading him.

"No future there."

They watched as Susan and Mia moved cots. Every time Mia bent and dragged a cot, her shirt exposed a taut midriff that caused a tightening in his own midriff.

Charlie cleared his throat. "What's wrong with right now?"

"We're both past that."

Mia looked their way and caught them watching her. "Get to work!" she called and, laughing, pointed to the coolers of food.

"How far past are you?" Charlie asked.

Kevin's breathing had gone shallow. He was hanging on to the edge of good sense by his fingernails. "Not far enough."

For the rest of the night, he watched Mia. She was in her element. The shelter had never run as efficiently. Susan was no slouch, but she'd always been overworked between getting all the supplies and doling them out. Kevin and others would pitch in when they could, but Mia provided the organization and efficiency that kept everyone's tempers in check. How could she look so out of place yet instantly fit in?

About 3:00 a.m., a wet and dirty Charlie dragged himself over to the coffee pot and chugged two cups while watching the activity in the shelter.

Thanks to the generators, the shelter had power and Kevin had cooked hot dogs donated by somebody. Charlie took one, plain, and stuffed half of it in his mouth. Chewing and swallowing, he gestured with the other half. "Look at those two." He meant Mia and Susan. "I tell you, it's a thing of beauty." Glancing at Kevin, he added, "That Mia looks to be a keeper."

"I haven't known her that long, Charlie."

"You've known her five hours longer than when I saw you last." Charlie reached for the mustard and squirted some on the rest of the hot dog. "And you didn't tell me I'm wrong."

"I know." Kevin stared across the room where Mia had just checked in a family with two little kids using the system she'd devised.

He'd been trying not to stare at her ever since Susan caught him and gave him a thumbs up sign. People had noticed him watching Mia, but he couldn't help it. His eyes just naturally sought her out and then he'd stop whatever he was doing and enjoy looking at her until somebody drew his attention away.

She was smart and sexy, a hard worker and, except for the fact that they were completely wrong for each other, just about perfect.

BY DAWN, MIA WAS exhausted, but happy. If she hadn't had something to do, she would have gone crazy. And Susan! Susan Chapman was the best resource manager Mia had ever worked with. After a couple of hours, they were practically reading each other's minds. Mia had already tried to convince Susan to come to Houston and work, but Susan liked living near the water.

Mia wasn't giving up yet.

At least thinking of ways to convince Susan to come work for Peck and Davilla helped distract Mia from thinking about Kevin, who stared at her all night as though he thought she was going to run off or break something.

Or…or as though he wanted to abandon the serving area and stalk across the room, sweep her into his arms and carry her off into the surf. Or the nearest bed. She stared at the cots surrounding her. Make that the nearest place where they could be alone.

Not that there was going to be an opportunity to be alone with him. Not while she kept imagining scenarios that involved Kevin and her together without clothes, usually bathed in the golden glow of a beach sunset. Yeah, she put herself right in the Cowboy Surfer pictures. The nude ones. With Kevin.

Honestly, she was not an exhibitionist.

Unless Kevin—no. Not happening. Or not happening

more than once—no. Not even once. That would be a mistake. Because… As Mia led a hungry family over to the food tables for breakfast, she met Kevin's gaze and forgot why flinging herself at him in surrender would be a mistake.

She could still feel his touch on the small of her back from when he'd introduced her to Susan hours ago. The instant it had happened, she'd wanted to curl herself against him and purr.

When Jonathan had kissed her it had been pretty good, certainly promising sexual compatibility down the road. But had the feeling of his lips lingered? No. Had his gaze felt as though he was actually touching her? No. Had she wanted to curl up and purr against *him?* Sadly, no. There had been awareness, but not on the visceral level of Kevin's appeal. Appeal? Such a wimpy word for the gnawing craving for him she felt.

No wonder Kevin had laughed at her theories of intelligent love. If she'd engaged Kevin in the same type of campaign with which she'd gone after Jonathan, there was no way she would have been able to protect her heart. The man made her bones melt with an impersonal touch—what would it feel like when the touch was personal?

She wanted to know. She wanted to know with an intensity that cut through fatigue and common sense.

So why couldn't she know? Nothing was stopping her, was it?

It was this sort of rationalizing that got people into trouble.

He glanced at her and didn't look away.

Neither did she.

She was in trouble.

Her heart pounded and prickles of awareness made her forget that a beach-town sandwich-shop owner wouldn't fit into her life and that she didn't want to fit into his. Gazing intently at each other wasn't going to do either of them any good.

Mia broke eye contact first and urged the soggy family forward.

Kevin greeted them with a ready smile, even though Mia hadn't seen him sit down since they'd arrived ten hours ago. The box meals they'd made at Kevin's restaurant had long since been consumed, but people kept bringing food from their fridges to share with those at the shelter. And Kevin had prepared the offerings, ensuring a constant smorgasbord was available for those who worked through the night.

"I'll bet I know what you'd like," he told the little boy of about seven. "How about a breakfast dog?"

The child laughed. "That's just a hot dog!"

"But you're eating it for breakfast, aren't you?"

The little boy, who had earlier appeared scared and sleepy, looked up at his parents, thrilled.

"Want some grape jelly on that?" Kevin asked.

He laughed. "Jelly on a hot dog is silly!"

"Have you eaten grape jelly on a hot dog before?"

The boy shook his head.

"Then how do you know it's silly?" Kevin squirted a small line of jelly down the hot dog and handed it to the boy.

He giggled uncertainly before biting into it. "Iss gud," he said, his mouth full.

The parents exchanged grateful looks with Kevin before accepting paper plates of scrambled eggs and day-old donuts along with cups of coffee.

Mia had stood by and watched as he'd diverted the little boy and now, all she wanted to do was drag the most perfect man in the universe back to the kitchen and have her way with him. Oh, wait. She didn't know if he was kind to animals, yet.

He caught her eye and winked.

"You're totally disgusting," she told him.

"Because of the grape jelly?"

"No. Because you're...perfect." She spat out the word. "How can you stand being so perfect?"

"O-o-okay. It's time for Mia to take a break."

"I'm fine." She ran both hands through the hair above her ears and fluffed it. "But it would be a lot easier if you had at least one flaw."

He pulled the empty scrambled-egg pan from the steam tray and replaced it with a fresh one. "I've got flaws."

Mia poured a cup of ice water from the dispenser and downed it in one gulp. "Name one."

He eyed her for several beats while wiping the serving area. "Sometimes I get an idea and act on it without taking time to consider the consequences."

"*Sometimes* you're impulsive. Oh. How. *Awful.*"

"It can be. Or it can be really great. Aren't you ever impulsive?"

"When I'm impulsive, I end up in a ditch." She filled her cup again and another one for Kevin. "Some people go with the flow and others plan the flow." She offered Kevin the cup. "I'm a planner." Except she hadn't planned the little jerk of her hand as his fingers brushed against hers when he took the flimsy paper cup, had she?

She should pretend it hadn't happened and stop staring at him as they drank the water. Or pretend she didn't notice that his eyes never left hers, either.

Silently, she held out her hand for the empty cup, and just as silently he handed it to her. She tossed their cups into the trash as he returned to wiping the counter, his movements slower and slower.

She watched, mesmerized, until without warning he slapped down the towel, grabbed her wrist, led her around the end of the table and pulled her into the kitchen. Stepping between two empty tray carts, he pushed her up against the pantry door and pressed his hard body against hers.

Mia's heart pounded. She'd better get one heck of a kiss out of this.

"I'm feeling impulsive," he said.

"I'm going to try going with the flow."

"Good plan." And he leaned in and kissed her.

Yes, it was one heck of a kiss. Not that she'd had any doubts.

Fire erupted between them. Mia's reaction was so immediate and so intense; it overpowered the details of his kiss. She was still responding to the anticipation of him kissing her, of his body pressed against hers just the way she'd wanted it to be since she realized whose body he had. Or rather who was inside the body.

How strange that she'd known the body before the man. How remarkable that the man was more attractive than the body.

How unlikely that they were devouring each other right at this very moment.

They'd skipped the preliminary teasing of a first kiss. Their mouths were open and their tongues frantically explored and stroked. She couldn't get close enough to him. Mia ran her hands over his back and clutched him to her.

This was chemistry as she'd never experienced chemistry before. Combustible. Boiling. Explosive. Addictive.

And there was nowhere to go with it.

Any second and someone would burst into the kitchen looking for them.

It seemed that Kevin had the same thought at the same time because he dragged his mouth from hers and rested his forehead against the top of her head. Breathing deeply, he gently rested a finger against her lips.

Mia kissed it softly and loosened her hold, her own breath pretty raggedy.

Her lips and cheeks stung from scraping against his beard. They'd be pink and anyone looking at her would know why. She didn't care.

Kevin stroked his thumb along her jaw.

She looked up, meeting his eyes for the first time since he'd dragged her in here. Moments passed as they each searched the other's gaze to discover if what had just happened was mutually earth-shaking.

Mia saw that and more. She saw wariness and something that surprised her. Loneliness. The man everybody knew and liked and admired was lonely.

Feeling a rush of affection, Mia stood on tiptoe and kissed his nose.

Laughing, Kevin backed away and took her hand. "C'mon. Let's get out of here."

But they only got as far as the main room before people had questions for her and more food donations for him.

During the hours that followed, Mia had time to wonder if Kevin had just meant getting out of the kitchen or leaving the shelter. Now that the passion had cooled, she could think objectively.

Yes, there was something potent between them, but was that enough to sustain a relationship?

Mia exhaled. She didn't want to think past kissing Kevin again and feeling his hands all over her and possibly—no probably, no absolutely sleeping with him. She didn't care if it didn't lead anywhere. This was the kind of hot, but short-lived combustibility that made people drop out of college for a semester so they could follow their idealistic boyfriends to Paraguay and live in a hut.

So, Mia thought philosophically, maybe she and Kevin should get together and let this thing burn itself out.

She swayed. Or maybe she should just get some sleep.

It was two o'clock on Saturday afternoon and Mia felt

dizzy and a little sick to her stomach. She'd been awake and working full-out since six o'clock Friday morning.

"I'm done," she told Kevin, who was washing dishes by hand. *Washing dishes!* "Even Susan is zonked out."

"I was wondering how long you'd keep going." He rinsed a cooking pot, put it on the draining rack and dried his hands. "I was ready to call it quits, oh, right after dawn."

And just like that, the memory of their kiss, burning encounter, whatever, zinged through her and gave her an energy boost—at least until she and Kevin loaded the empty ice chests into his truck and started back to the restaurant.

The storm had passed and the sun was out, steaming the wet sand and streets. Debris, both natural and man-made was everywhere. Although the tide had receded, a line of trash illustrated how far it had come in.

"I'd like to check on your car later, if you don't mind."

Mia shook her head. "I'm too tired to drive back home anyway."

"You can sleep at my place. And I gotta tell you, as good as kissing you was earlier, I mean *sleep* sleep."

"That's the most romantic thing you could have said."

His smile lit up his tired face. "There isn't going to be any power yet," he told her. "Anytime there're high winds, the city cuts off the power so downed lines won't fall into the water and electrocute people. The crews will have to inspect and make repairs before they turn it back on."

"You're saying no air conditioning." Mia positioned her face over the vent in the truck.

"I've got a window unit in the bedroom hooked up to the generator. It's the only room that'll be cool."

"Is this your gentlemanly way of saying that we'll be sleeping in the same bed?"

"Only if you want air conditioning. 'Cause I do and I'm

not gentlemanly enough to offer to sleep on the sofa in the front room."

"But you're gentlemanly enough to offer to share your bed."

"I'm definitely that kind of gentleman."

They pulled up at Kevin's Patio. The restaurant had escaped with just a little cosmetic damage except that one of the awning roofs was sagging because a support pole had broken. As they walked by, Kevin pointed out streaks of blue paint. "Looks like a car hit it."

"And they didn't leave a note?"

"Mia." He gestured all around them.

"Okay, sorry. I wasn't thinking."

"I've had worse happen during spring break." He and Mia unloaded the truck and she was so tired, she had to concentrate on putting one foot in front of the other. And she wasn't doing too well with that.

Kevin noticed her stumble. "I'll put this stuff away if you want to hit the bathroom first. I'm planning on a shower and then sleeping around the clock."

"A shower sounds heavenly."

It felt heavenly, too. Afterwards, a somewhat revived Mia went back downstairs to tell Kevin she was out of the shower, but didn't find him. Hearing noises in the restaurant area, she left the kitchen and found a couple of cars parked in front, and people looking through the windows.

"Are you open?" a man called when he saw her.

Were they? Mia didn't think they had any food, but Kevin was the one to make the decision. "Let me check."

When she stepped out back where he'd parked the truck, she heard running water and followed the sound to an outdoor shower customers could use to rinse off sand and salt water. It was rustic, to be generous, with walls on two sides and open to the ocean.

And Kevin was in it, standing with his eyes closed, head thrown back, and totally naked, visible to anyone who happened to be passing by on the beach. Fortunately, no one was.

Mia stared, unable to help herself. He was every bit as gorgeous in the flesh as he'd been in his pictures.

She sighed, a long quivering sigh. She wanted him in a way she'd never wanted any other man. Even though there was no future for them, she still wanted him. It was inevitable. The best she could do was try not to get hurt too much. She liked him a whole lot. Maybe that would be enough and she wouldn't have to fall in love with him. That would be really bad. It would take her a long time to get over loving Kevin.

Silently returning to the front of the restaurant, she informed the people that they were indeed closed, made sure the Closed sign was visible and headed back to Kevin in the shower.

She approached from the beach side and watched as he rinsed soap out of his hair. Suds trailed over his shoulders and down his back, continuing over his hips and bumping along the hair on his legs.

Mia couldn't look away. She should say something, at least let him know she was there.

But she didn't and when he opened his eyes as he slicked back his hair, he didn't react when he saw her. He'd probably known she was watching him.

Holding her gaze with his, he turned off the water and toweled off.

"I never slept with Jonathan," Mia told him, as though they'd been discussing it. "And I'm not sure I would have this weekend, either. But I am sure that I'm never going to because I'm through with Jonathan." She gave Kevin a crooked smile. "You've spoiled me for other men."

Without waiting for his response, assuming he had a response, Mia went back inside and up the stairs where she collapsed onto Kevin's bed in the blessed cool from the window unit.

5

WEARING A TOWEL HE held at the waist, Kevin entered his bedroom. She'd gone and done it now. The one thing—the *one* thing—that might have saved him from losing his heart to Mia was knowing she was involved with that dog, Jonathan Black.

And now she'd wiped it all away, leaving Kevin defenseless.

He steeled himself and glanced at his bed. A fully-clothed, sleepy-eyed Mia lifted her hand in a lazy wave.

Kevin pulled open a drawer and rummaged through it for a pair of boxer shorts and a T-shirt.

Mia yawned. "Do you always sleep in boxers?"

"Nope."

"Then don't bother on my account."

He slid a look toward her. "Do you always sleep fully dressed?"

"Nope."

"Then don't bother on my account."

"I didn't want to presume."

"Please. Presume all you want." Kevin walked into the bathroom and hung up his towel.

He was too tired to fight his desire, but too tired to do anything about it with any finesse, either.

He rubbed the stubble on his face. Shaving could wait. Walking over to the bed, he stared down at Mia. Her eyes were closed as she fumbled with the buttons on her blouse.

Exhaling a sigh from deep within, Kevin opened the door to all the feelings he'd been trying to keep out and let them wash through him. He felt a connection with this woman and he wanted to explore it, even though he was setting himself up for a world of hurt.

She'd had a point about being smart in love, although he hadn't wanted to admit it. And this wasn't smart. This was the city girl/country boy conflict of his marriage all over again.

Mia half opened her eyes. "You're so beautiful," she murmured sleepily. "Inside, too."

Nuts. Kevin sat on the bed beside her and took over for her fumbling fingers. He unbuttoned her blouse and unsnapped the front of her shorts. Mia wiggled out of both and lay back down, her creamy skin more than living up to the way he'd imagined it through the wet dress.

"You're wearing some mighty fine undies," he said. Pale pink with gray embroidery in the lace on basically invisible fabric.

"Do you think they're sexy?"

"Yeah. But useless. Can I take them off?"

"Okay. They're not hiding anything anyway."

"No, they're not," he agreed. But he still enjoyed peeling them off her.

"That's right. You're a skin man, aren't you?" she asked as they lay down.

"There's no substitute for a naked woman cuddled up against me." He drew her into the curve of his body. She settled next to him and her breathing slowed. Kevin listened to her fall asleep within a half-dozen breaths, kissed her gently on the shoulder and passed out.

MOONLIGHT STREAMED INTO the room when Mia awoke. Kevin wasn't beside her and she had no idea what time it was. On her way to the bathroom, the hum of the AC unit changed as the compressor kicked in. Cool air blew across her body reminding her that she was naked, giving her a last-minute heads-up that if she didn't intend to have sex with Kevin, now would be the time to put on clothes.

Not only was she not going to put on clothes, she wasn't going to get back under the sheet, either. She lay on the bed. Wise or not, she was ready.

She heard Kevin on the stairs and sat up as the glow of a flashlight preceded him into the room.

"What time is it?"

"A little after one." He handed her a chilled water bottle.

She hadn't known she was thirsty until that very moment. "One in the morning? That's a weird time to wake up. It's too early to get up and I don't feel like going back to sleep."

"I'm thinking it's the perfect time." He climbed into the bed bringing a citrusy scent with him.

"You shaved." Mia cracked open the bottle.

"Didn't want to rough up all that gorgeous skin." He leaned on one elbow and watched as she drained half the water bottle at once.

The light kissed the planes of his body, reminding her of the matted photographs against the wall. Studying him, she sighed a little when she realized that the pictures hadn't required much retouching. His chest was smooth and his skin was bare all the way to his lower abdomen. At the juncture of his legs, hair a darker blond than his surfer locks surrounded his growing erection. She smiled. *That* hadn't been in the pictures.

"Moonlight is a good look for you," she told him.

"Naked is a good look for you," he said.

Mia carefully set the water bottle on the window ledge and hugged her knees. "Do you think it'll be the same? You know, between us? Like before?"

"You mean so instantly intense and hot and urgent that you have no control?" His eyes glittered in the silver light.

Mia's skin tingled and her heart beat in heavy thuds she could feel throughout her body. "Yeah. Like that."

"I hope so," he said and reached for her.

They met in a tangle of arms and legs, frantically grasping for each other, their mouths fusing together.

And like their earlier kiss, the heat was instant and all-consuming. But it wasn't exactly the same as before. This time, skin was involved. Lots and lots of lovely skin. Mia shuddered and ran her hands over Kevin's body as he touched her, *here, there and everywhere,* she thought a bit hysterically. When she could think. Which wasn't often. Or necessary.

Feeling was necessary. Feeling was good. Feeling was everything.

Feeling drove her; the heat consumed her. He stole her breath and gave her his own. Sensation overwhelmed her nerve endings. His touch was too much and not enough at the same time, a burning cold that made her breath come in shallow pants.

"More!" she pleaded, depending on Kevin to figure out what she meant.

Kevin stroked her from thigh to shoulder and back again. His movements were jerky. She'd take them.

They were beyond a gentle, teasing exploration. Beyond a slow seduction. Kevin touched her all over, claiming her, imprinting her with his taste and scent. And Mia gave as good as she got.

"I can't get enough of you." His rough voice was heavy

with lust and wonder. And then he nipped her earlobe, a tiny sharp prick that increased the ache between her legs.

Gasping, she arched her neck. Kevin opened his mouth over the pulse that beat in her throat and sucked hard.

Her belly tightened. "You're not getting ready to pop out a set of fangs, are you?"

He dragged his mouth away, looking down at her, gaze unfocused, breathing fast. "Do you want me to?"

"What would happen if I said 'yes'?"

"I'd distract you like this." He licked his way to her breast, his tongue trailing that icy fire, swirling it over her nipple. When he pulled the tip into his mouth, she nearly came off the bed.

"Ke..." She couldn't even form his entire name. She couldn't breathe.

She was mindless with need.

And thoroughly distracted.

This was not the way Mia Weiss had experienced sex, with her body bending and thrusting all on its own as she selfishly sought her own pleasure. And there were supposed to be stages to go through, levels of arousal where there was mutual pleasure in giving and taking. More control. Less grabbing and flailing.

Actually, Mia was doing all the flailing and grabbing. Kevin was doing all the sucking and stroking and teasing.

And she was fine with that.

At least until the tension coiling within her caused one of her flailing arms to smack against the bedside table.

She moaned with two kinds of frustration.

Kevin lifted his mouth. "You okay?"

"No, but I will be more than okay if I can just get to that condom."

"I'll get—"

"No!" She pushed his head back to her chest. "Do not

stop. Do not take your hands or mouth off me. I will deal with the condom."

"It's been a while, but best I can remember, I'm supposed to wear the condom." His voice was muffled, since his mouth was full of breast.

"I know that!" she groaned.

Her fingers closed over a packet. She tore it open with her teeth and managed to rip the contents. "Tell me you've got more," she sobbed.

"I've got more." His hand left her breast for a few seconds that seemed like hours. "And even if I didn't, there are dispensers in the public restrooms downstairs. A day at the beach should be fun, not a mistake you pay for for the rest of your life."

"You're such a responsible person!" she wailed, not sure why she was crying and not caring much, either.

He loosened her clenched fist and slipped the ring of latex beneath her fingers, and then his mouth and both hands were touching her again and she stopped sobbing.

His fingers stroked between her legs and her hips bucked. Gentling his fingers, he slid them slowly over her as the tension inside her formed a knot of pure need.

She was close, so very close, but she wanted him with her.

"Please," she whispered, fumbling between them.

He captured her hand. "Tell me." The words were rough. "Tell me what you need."

"You. Inside me. Now!"

Passion glazed his features and he blinked down at her as though he had trouble processing the words.

"It wasn't a request!"

And he plunged into her, fast and hard. She gasped, clutching at him and only then realized that her hand was empty. He hadn't been processing her words, he'd been processing the condom.

He takes direction well, Mia thought. Then she wrapped her legs around him and hung on for the ride.

It was a short ride, like one loop on a roller coaster. She climbed to the top, felt suspended in air for a few breathless moments of anticipation and then let go and whooshed back to earth, trembling in the glorious aftermath.

Mia gulped air. That was quick. Intense, but quick. Her body throbbed as the fire between them became more like glowing embers and less like a raging, all-consuming inferno. But it was still there ready to flare again.

Her breathing slowed and deepened, matching Kevin's. He was above her, balancing some of his weight on his arms. Mia wanted his entire body against her, pressing her into the bed.

She shifted and he flinched. Her eyes flew open as she became horribly aware that Kevin hadn't been on the roller coaster with her, as it were.

"I'm sorry," she whispered.

"For being so bossy?" She heard the strain in his voice.

"I'm not bossy!" But she had been really insistent. And selfishly unaware. And a pretty rotten lover, when it came down to it.

He gave a tense chuckle. "You do know what you want."

"What I *wanted* was for our first time to be together," she explained.

He kissed her. "Our first time's not over yet."

A thrill of anticipation shot through Mia.

Eyes locked on hers Kevin began moving again, slower this time, deeper, more deliberate.

"I don't believe this," she said as the heat began to build. "I never—"

"You're complaining?" He picked up the pace.

"No. Oh, no. No, no, no-o-o-o." In fact, Mia was going to stop talking now. Thinking, too. She moved her hips upward to meet his thrusts and watched his eyes grow heavy-lidded with lust before he buried his head next to hers.

She gripped his sweat-slickened back as he drove into her, taking them both up an even higher roller-coaster hill. Again there was that moment when everything stilled before he sent them careening over the edge.

Mia heard him saying her name, over and over and couldn't tell where his shuddering stopped and hers began. She felt dizzy. She was going to black out. There was a limit to how much pleasure the human body could endure and she'd reached hers. And then she gasped because she'd been holding her breath and the dizziness receded.

"Mia," he breathed.

Mia drew in air. "Is—is it always like this for you?"

Balancing himself on his arms, Kevin brushed his lips across her temple. "It's never like this. So when it is, we need to pay attention."

She didn't want to pay attention. She wanted to savor and enjoy and…enjoy a few more times before they parted with some fabulous memories. "Maybe it's just a chemical thing and it'll burn itself out."

Kevin gave her a slow smile. "We've got a few hours before dawn. How about we test your theory?"

6

EVERYTHING LOOKED different in the morning and not just because golden sunlight had replaced the silvery glow of the moon.

Mia lay on her back and stared at the sliver of cloudless blue sky she could see out the top of the window behind the bed.

Now what?

She'd been awake wondering for a while. Kevin had been asleep, but sometime within the past fifteen minutes or so, he'd rolled onto his back, too, no doubt thinking the same thing she was, which was where did they go from here? Or did they go from here?

Kevin brushed his fingers against her hand and slowly, gently linked his little finger around hers. A tiny point of contact, but it warmed her as they lay there.

Do not fall in love with this man, she told herself fiercely. *Do not mistake great sex for love.*

You don't have great sex without love said an inner voice.

She was supposed to have been protecting her heart. What had happened? She wasn't supposed to fall in love with Kevin. She didn't want to live at the beach and she knew Kevin didn't want to leave. The rhythm of the ocean was part of his soul. He wouldn't be happy away from it. He wouldn't be the same person. As for her moving here—forget it. The slow, laid-back lifestyle wasn't for her. She thrived on urban energy. She'd go nuts living here. They'd end up hating each other.

She *knew* this. He knew this. Unfortunately, her heart didn't.

Why was the right man so wrong for her?

NOW WHAT?

Kevin could hear Mia's thoughts as though she said them aloud.

He didn't want to let her go, but he wouldn't ask her to stay. Never again would he ask a woman to change her life for him.

This was gonna hurt. He'd known he was doomed from the moment he'd kissed her and bells had gone off as though he'd hit the jackpot at the Grand Casino. Actually, he'd known earlier when she'd started running things at the shelter. The kiss had confirmed it.

Beside him, Mia inhaled deeply and let out her breath.

One of them needed to say something. This was his house, his bed, he was the man. It was up to him. He turned his head on the pillow without knowing what he was going to say.

Mia turned her head, too. If Kevin had seen love blazing from her eyes, he might have said one thing, but when he saw a cautious wariness and a frozen expression that told him she was bracing herself, he said the only thing he could. "Ready to go get your car?"

THE DRIVE TO WHERE her car sat took about a third of the time it had taken on Friday night.

Other than idle comments about the condition of the road

and the mess and household debris that had ended up far from the beach houses, Mia and Kevin were silent.

She almost hoped her car needed repair so she'd have an excuse to stay another night, but other than a dented right rear quarter panel that Kevin pulled out so it wouldn't rub against the wheel, it started right up.

"I don't think you bent the frame," he said as he chipped sea grass and dried mud off her bumper. "But get it checked out sooner rather than later."

"I will, thanks." She opened the trunk and wrinkled her nose at the sour smell.

Kevin reached around her and felt the carpeting. Mia closed her eyes when the heat of his body made her want to lean into him and bury her face in that wonderful spot where his neck met his shoulder.

"Just damp. Air it out and you should be okay."

The car might be okay. Mia had doubts about herself.

He closed the trunk, avoiding eye contact with her even though her clothes were dry this time. "Let's put your bag in the backseat."

He opened the door and pulled the bag from her unresisting fingers. Her heart pounded and she hated the way she felt.

This weekend hadn't been real life. It wasn't even Kevin's real life. She'd get over him. She had to.

The door slammed shut, both on the car and on their time together.

She turned to face him and found him staring at her, his jaw rigid. So he felt the same way she did.

At least they didn't need to have the talk.

"I'll never forget you," Mia said.

"I will always remember you," he told her, and it sounded better than what she'd said.

She got into her car.

"Follow me and I'll lead you back to the main road."

He closed her door. He stood there a moment, his fingertips touching the window glass. Then he strode back to his truck.

Mia followed him along a complicated route of unpaved roads she didn't remember driving on before, and guessed that he was avoiding places that were still impassable. She never would have found her way on her own.

When they turned onto a two-lane asphalt road, signs told Mia the main highway was just ahead. Kevin pulled over to the side of the road and waved Mia on.

This was it. She drove alongside and lifted her hand in a farewell gesture Kevin didn't see because he stared straight ahead.

She hesitated, but he didn't look over at her.

Mia slowly rolled the car forward as everything inside her screamed that leaving was a huge mistake. Only it wasn't. The mistake would be staying.

But she couldn't make her foot press the car's accelerator. Her skin felt tight as though her emotions had grown too big for it to contain.

She didn't want to feel this say-anything-do-anything-just-don't-leave-me desperation. She didn't like feeling that life as she knew it wasn't worth living without Kevin.

She didn't want anyone having that kind of power over her. She didn't want her *emotions* having that kind of power over her. Not healthy. Not good.

This was the beginning of obsession.

And still she couldn't drive away.

She turned off the car and flung open the door, storming back to the truck. Kevin was already jogging toward her.

"I… Love's whomped me upside the head!" she wailed.

He folded his arms around her. "I know, I know. Me, too."

"But you didn't say anything!" she sobbed into his shoulder. "You were going to let me drive off!" She hated that she was crying and whining. It was pointless and distracting and embarrassing. And she couldn't stop.

"Mia, I want you in my life. But I don't know how that can happen. There's nothing for you here. You'd be bored out of your mind."

"There's you."

He kissed her gently on the lips. Gentle was a new thing for them. She liked it. For variety.

"I can't be somebody's whole life." Emotion scraped his words into a rough whisper.

Oh, no. She'd be begging next. She gritted her teeth to stop the words.

Fortunately, he continued, "Don't think I haven't been trying to figure out a way you could work with Susan in City Services, or find somebody or something you can organize, but life here is real different than your life in Houston."

Mia stopped crying. *Susan.* She'd liked working with Susan. Susan was more a big-picture person and Mia was a detail person and one of those details triggered a thought about the big picture.

Sniffling, she brushed at the corners of her eyes and raised her head. "You know," she began carefully. "You said you want me in your life, but you didn't say anything about being in *my* life."

"I don't—"

"Know anything about my life?" she finished for him.

His mouth tightened. "I had a couple of meetings at the Peck and Davilla offices. I've dealt with the people at the beach house before."

"And based on that, you think you know my whole life?"

"Based on a stormy weekend, you think you know mine?"

They stared at each other. "Even so," Kevin said after a moment, "my business is here."

"And my front door is about an hour, hour-and-a-half drive from the spot where we're standing now. It's not thousands of miles away in the thin air of the mountains. Trust me, there's plenty of thick, humid air in Houston for you to breathe."

Kevin's face eased and he laughed softly. "We may be over thinking this. We don't have to make permanent decisions immediately." He cupped her cheek. "I don't suppose you'd be interested in a weekend job selling boxed meals to tourists?"

Mia smiled. "I've been looking for a way to earn extra gas money. I kinda, sorta like this guy who lives in the area."

"Then you're hired." He looped his arms around her waist and Mia felt herself beaming up at him.

"Now, I wonder if you can help me with another problem," he said. "The Chamber of Commerce wants to draw tourists back to the area. It's been rough since Hurricane Ike. I'm considering volunteering to be the representative to the regional tourism board that meets in Houston. I kinda, sorta have a thing for a woman who lives there and it would be a good excuse to see her."

"You probably don't need an excuse."

"But I will need somewhere to stay. Any recommendations?"

This might work. This might really work. "I've got a place in mind. Are there a lot of meetings?"

"All the time."

"But you could just drive back home after them."

"Not after wining and dining convention organizers and the media until all hours. That wouldn't be responsible of me," he said solemnly.

"You are to be commended for recognizing that." Mia was having difficulty maintaining a straight face. Hope and happiness had grabbed her heart and were jumping up and down. "Before you officially volunteer, you should check out the place where you'll stay."

"Absolutely. When?"

"How does right now sound?"

Kevin's wide smile answered her before he did. "I've got no electricity and no food. Now sounds perfect."

Safe Text

1

"DUDE. GIVE IT UP."

"Stop calling me dude." Gil Shaughnessy kept his gaze on the woman sitting at her desk at the opposite end of the hallway, past the deserted cubicle village.

Beside him, his partner, Paul, slung a messenger bag crosswise over his chest. "Man, you are entering stalker territory."

"I have no idea what you're talking about."

"You." Paul gestured down the hall. "Watching her."

He meant Cammy Philips, Jonathan Black's assistant. "I'm not watching her."

"You're standing in the doorway so you can see her."

"I'm stretching my legs."

"That's just sick."

"Stretching my legs?"

"The way you look at her. You know the way Cammy looks at Jonathan? With that puppy-dog adoration? If she had a tail, she'd wag it."

Gil knew.

"That's the way you look at her."

Gil interrupted his Cammy surveillance to shoot a warning glare at Paul.

"Don't glower at me. You know I'm telling you the truth."

"'Glower'? When did *glower* enter your vocabulary?"

"It was in the script for that cell-phone ad we shot."

Gil hadn't expected Paul to answer.

"See, I read that the dad was supposed to glower at the daughter for using too many minutes but I thought it was a typo and they meant glow."

"Is *that* why you used glitter pens on the story boards?"

"Yeah. I thought maybe he was getting the message about the better cell-phone plan from, you know." Paul pointed upward. "On high."

"I think *you* were high."

"No, but sniffing those glitter pens will give you a buzz. Anyway, glow*er.* Lowered brows, stern expression, chin down." He gestured to Gil. "Yep. Just like that."

Gil crossed his arms over his chest and directed his glower toward Cammy Philips.

"Gil... Go home, man. Have you seen how dark it's getting out there? You know once the rain starts all the usual places will flood. It's rush hour and the traffic will be a mess. Do you really want to spend your Friday evening trying to get home? Or even worse, get trapped here and be forced to work?"

"I'm sticking around until she leaves."

"Spoken like a true stalker."

"Knock it off, Paul."

Paul joined him in the doorway. "Why don't you just make your move?"

Gil shook his head. "She'll never go out with me as long as she has a chance with Jonathan."

"She has no chance with Jonathan."

"I'm waiting for her to realize that."

"And how long have you been waiting?"

Gil didn't want to think about it. "Couple of years."

"Closer to three. I know, because that's how long we've been partners, which, coincidentally, is when Cammy became Jonathan's assistant."

"Your point?"

"Move on."

Good advice. Great advice. But… "I can't. I *know* she's going to give up on Jonathan. He's *using* her."

"Of course he is! She's the most over-qualified assistant in the history of Peck and Davilla. He owes his last two promotions to her and he knows it. Do you think he's going to jeopordize that? Hell, no. He's going to string her along for as long as he can."

Gil hated that Paul was right. "Eventually, Jonathan will mess up and when he does, I'm going to be right there with a shoulder for Cammy to cry on."

Out of the corner of his eye, he saw Paul shake his head. "You'll be rebound guy."

"Don't care." So what if she was crying on his shoulder? At least he'd be holding her in his arms, something he'd fantasized about often.

Gil was stuck and he knew it. She was The One. Other women didn't do it for him. Cammy had pushed the pause button on his love life the same way Jonathan had paused hers.

"People are starting to talk," Paul said.

Gil straightened in surprise. "About me and Cammy?"

"No. Just about you. They think you're gay."

"Oh." Gil slouched against the door jamb again.

"Man, do you hear yourself? What I don't get is why you didn't hook up with her when she was your partner."

"*Because* she was my partner. It was tricky. I was laying groundwork."

"And?"

"We never got off the ground. She was blinded by the dazzling sun that is Jonathan Black."

"Not that you're bitter. Okay, lecture over." Paul moved into the hallway. "I'm outta here." He took two steps before pivoting. "I will say that lately, you haven't been at the top of your game. That means you and I haven't been a winning team. I like to win, so snap out of it."

Gil met his partner's eyes. "Understood."

"Later, man." Paul's path to the elevators blocked Gil's view of Cammy.

Probably on purpose.

Paul was right about everything he'd said. Gil was only surprised that he hadn't brought it up before. He knew he hadn't been on top of his game, as Paul put it, but watching Jonathan play Cammy made his teeth hurt.

How could someone as smart as Cammy be so dumb about Jonathan?

They'd both started at P&D at the same time and had been randomly paired. It was a good pairing, even though they were both copywriters and neither of them could sketch worth a darn. But Cammy was freakishly adept at anticipating what a client wanted, even if it wasn't what the client asked for.

Together they made creative magic, so it wasn't long before Gil wondered if that would translate into physical magic.

But was finding out worth possibly wrecking their creative partnership?

Cammy never indicated a romantic interest in Gil, and he'd searched pretty hard for signs. It became disappointingly clear that Cammy wasn't suppressing hidden desires because they worked together; she just didn't think of him that way.

So carefully, slowly, Gil set out to get her attention. During brainstorming sessions, he slipped in questions about her personal likes and dislikes on everything from men's clothing and hair styles to whether she preferred oil and vinegar or cream-based salad dressings.

And yes, he kept a spreadsheet which Paul didn't know about.

The result was that Gil now wore khakis and pale blue button-down shirts exclusively, styled his hair a little longer than he preferred and became a connoisseur of balsamic vinegars. He gave up wearing contacts when she complimented his heavy black "retro" glasses one day. They weren't retro so much as old, and he only wore them then because he'd been up all night and contacts irritated his eyes.

Gil was engaged in a subliminal advertising campaign with Cammy as his target market. All he'd lacked was the catalyst that would cause her to see him in a different way and put that gleam of awareness in her eyes.

As it turned out, the catalyst was their transfer to Jonathan Black's department and the gleam in Cammy's eyes was for Jonathan.

He had that effect on women, although Gil couldn't see why. Jonathan dazzled them and they were never the same again.

Frankly, they were a lot stupider.

Cammy was the perfect example. She broke up their team to take an intern-level job as Jonathan's assistant even though it meant a cut in pay and status.

Three years later, Gil's salary was double what it had been, and he and Paul had their own accounts and shared an office. Not a large one, but they'd moved out of Cubicle City.

Cammy didn't even rate a cubicle. She sat at a desk in the fourth-floor client-display gallery, which Jonathan had turned into his private reception area. Nice.

Gil saw Cammy turn to look at the wall clock behind her and quietly cross the hallway to the conference room.

Jonathan's meeting was running into dinnertime and Cammy was probably checking to see if they wanted her to order something. She shouldn't even be here at this hour. She wasn't getting paid overtime.

When she returned to her desk, she didn't immediately pick up the phone, so Gil invented an excuse to walk down the hallway.

"Hey, Cammy." Gil's overly casual tone masked the state of hyperawareness he was in every time he interacted with her.

"Gil?" She barely acknowledged him. "I didn't know you were still here."

"I was hoping to catch Ross when he got out of the meeting. Any idea when it'll finish?"

"They just took a break, but they're not ordering food, so it'll be soon."

Gil made a show of checking his watch, pulling back his cuff to reveal the brown leather strap because Cammy preferred leather straps over metal ones. "They're running late for a Friday. I'm surprised Jonathan asked you to stay."

She glanced at him. "Oh, he didn't ask, but I know he appreciates it when I do."

How? How do you know he appreciates it? Because of a smile and an offhand "Thanks, babe, you're the best"? Do you realize you gave away three hours of your life and he doesn't even notice and he'll never notice because you're not his type? You're my type. But Gil said nothing. She wouldn't have listened anyway.

Instead, he went for the tried and true to extend his excuse to talk with her. "The weather is looking rotten."

"Is it?"

"Yeah." He glanced around pointedly. "I guess you can't see out a window from here."

She rolled her chair around and brought up her computer. "That's what weather-cam and traffic-cam sites are for."

They both watched as live video of the Southwest Freeway appeared. Cars were already running with their lights on, forming a solid ribbon of traffic. WEATHER ALERT: FLASH FLOOD WARNING scrolled across the bottom of the video. A tiny weather-radar picture was in the corner.

Gil leaned forward. "Hey, click on that."

She did and the radar changed to full screen. They stared at the approaching lines of thunderstorms.

"I'm going to zoom out." Cammy clicked until the whole state and the Gulf of Mexico was visible. A swirling pinwheel of clouds sat off the coast of Northern Mexico.

"The hurricane's not that strong, but it sure got big," Gil said. "And we're on the wet side. I hope it moves inland and doesn't sit there and dump a bunch of water on us."

"I know." Cammy sighed and straightened, forcing Gil to back up a little. "When it rains hard, our apartment parking-lot entrance floods. We have to leave our cars on the street or we can't get in and out."

"What a pain. You should move," he told her.

"Can't. That's why my rent is low."

I own a house. I own a house because I didn't spend the last three years working for peanuts. Gil looked down at her as Cammy checked more traffic reports. She'd like his house. Contemporary, clean lines, neutral colors. Her style.

"Shall I tell Ross you're looking for him?" she asked.

Gil shook his head. "It'll wait until Monday."

Walking back to his office, he marveled that Cammy could be so obtuse. He got her to admit that she was working unpaid overtime, probably unnecessarily, and pointed out the approaching bad weather. And still she stayed.

And so Gill stayed, too. And when she did leave, he'd follow her car to make sure she got home okay. He wouldn't tell her, and as long as the Jonathan dazzle was in her eyes, she wouldn't notice.

2

IT WAS RAINING SO HARD, Cammy could hear it blowing against the windows through the closed door of Jonathan's office.

When she'd seen the meeting break up, she'd straightened her desk and had gathered her things, but Jonathan was still talking to the client in the conference room. Cammy left her computer on and watched live radar, since it was raining so hard the street cameras only showed white foggy images.

Normally, she'd wait out the worst of it, but all the forecasts predicted a long night of storms. It was funny—well, not funny to the people experiencing it—but a monster hurricane could be a hundred miles away to the east and not a drop of rain would fall in Houston, but a weak one three hundred miles to the southwest could soak the area.

Cammy wasn't looking forward to driving home in the dark and possibly being surprised by deep water. She knew to avoid freeway underpasses and which roads on her route usually flooded, but with Houston's constant construction, drainage patterns changed and would catch people off guard.

And she was hungry. Maybe…maybe Jonathan would suggest they grab a sandwich and sit out the traffic together. Or maybe, since it was a weekend, he'd take her to dinner.

Oh, wait, no. The beach house. She'd reserved the beach house for him. But he wouldn't drive down there tonight, would he?

The very moment Cammy had the thought, Jonathan burst from the conference room. Alone. He stopped short when he saw her and in the seconds before her presence registered, he looked shell-shocked.

So the meeting had not gone well. Was still not going well. She'd have to—

"Cammy!" His faced eased into a Jonathan smile, yet his eyes looked a little wild. "What are you doing here?"

"Staying until you finish your meeting." *As I always do.*

He shoved a hand into his pocket and withdrew his cell phone. "I didn't mean for you to do that. Go on. I'll see you later."

"Okay." Cammy turned off her computer and Jonathan headed back to the conference room.

How strange. She wondered about it as she made her way to the parking garage.

When she emerged from the elevator on the top floor, rainy mist sprayed her from the moment the door opened. The security lights glowed pinkly as the wind blew sheets of water across the uncovered roof.

The only truly bad part of being Jonathan's assistant was that she was considered a junior-level employee and assigned to the rooftop. She'd hinted to Jonathan that she'd been parking up here for three years, but nothing had come of his assurance that he'd "see what he could do."

Standing under the overhang, Cammy stared at the four cars left on the roof. Hers was in the middle on the outer row, the perfect position for getting scoured by gusts of rain-laden wind. At least it was a free car wash.

She had an umbrella, not that it would do any good. Slipping off her shoes, she stuffed them into her purse. She kept her keys at the ready, waiting for a lull in the wind. Getting wet was a given, but she didn't want to get blown over.

As minutes passed and the rain didn't lessen, Cammy considered returning to the office. Peck and Davilla had a break room with cots and she could even spend the night there. But due to the weather and the weekend, the building was nearly deserted and she'd be the only one on the fourth floor. Not good. Unless Jonathan decided to stay, but even Cammy wasn't that desperate.

The elevator dinged and she was surprised to see Gil emerge. She'd forgotten that he was still working in his office. "What are you doing up here?" She had to raise her voice to be heard above the storm's noise.

He blinked as mist speckled his glasses. Removing them, he dried the lenses on his shirt. "Somebody was in my spot this morning, so I parked up here."

"Did you report their license number to Human Resources?"

He glanced up. His eyes looked exposed without the heavy glasses. His face seemed longer and thinner, too. It was a nice face, Cammy thought. Husband handsome her friends would say. The glasses gave him a completely different look.

"It's no big deal," he said.

That was generous of him because people were extremely territorial over their parking spots.

Putting his glasses back on, he surveyed the lot. "Not letting up?"

"There hasn't been a break yet. Which car is yours?"

"The black RAV4 over by the wall."

"At least you're sheltered from the wind. I'm right out there in the open." She pointed to her little red Kia.

"I don't think it matters. We're going to get wet no matter what."

The roaring of the rain echoed in the parking garage.

Cammy clutched her purse to her chest. "I'm ready to make a run for it." She walked to the edge of the overhang.

Gil touched her arm, shouting above the noise. "I'll follow you out."

Cammy nodded. "Okay. One...two...three!" She ran into the rain and was instantly soaked. She kept running to her car anyway, opening it with her remote so all she had to do was grab the door and fling herself in.

Slamming the door closed, she exhaled. Her bangs dripped water into her eyes. Brushing them aside, she checked in the rearview mirror for the black car parked behind her. Gil was already inside.

Cammy arranged her wet slacks so they didn't pull and put her shoes back on. After fastening her seat belt, she turned the key in the ignition.

Nothing happened.

She tried again. There was a click. Maybe. With the rain pounding on her car, it was difficult to hear. She tried again, but nothing. The engine wasn't even turning over.

Obviously some critical component didn't like the rain. Great. Just great. She rested her head on the steering wheel for a moment, and then dug out her cell phone. Not that she had high hopes for prompt roadside assistance in this weather.

Gil's black SUV pulled in beside her. "Are you all right?" he mouthed through the window.

She shook her head and he gestured for her to unlock the passenger door.

Seconds later, he sat in her car dripping water everywhere and bringing the scent of wet cotton and a different brand of fabric softener than she used. His shoulders extended past the edge of the seat and Cammy's car suddenly seemed very, very small.

"Won't start?" he asked.

She shook her head as he reached across her to turn the

key, tilting his head to listen. His arm was inches away from her thigh, which…bothered her. Cammy eased her leg away.

Gil had her depress the accelerator while he cranked the engine again. Then he straightened, carefully withdrawing his arm to avoid accidentally touching her, she noticed. Well, that was awkward.

"My guess is that something got damp and needs to dry out."

No kidding. She gave him a contemptuous look. "Ya think?"

Gil peered at her through his rain spattered glasses. She immediately felt guilty. He was a nice guy just trying to help. "I'm sorry. I shouldn't have snapped at you."

He let a couple of beats go by. "No, you shouldn't have. You're angry and frustrated and you took it out on me."

True, but she'd expected him to brush off her apology, not scold her. When they'd been partners he'd never scolded her. It wasn't as though she hadn't apologized right away.

Once again, he took off the black glasses to dry them, except there wasn't anywhere dry on his shirt. He tugged a little fabric out from his waist band and drew her attention to his flat stomach and the way his wet khakis were molded to his thighs. When she realized she was staring at his lap, she jerked her gaze northward to check out the rest of him. His shirt clung damply revealing the broad shoulders she'd noticed earlier and a set of nicely muscled arms. Where had he been hiding those?

Gil wiped his glasses with long, elegant fingers. Long, elegant, ringless fingers.

They'd spent a lot of hours together when they'd been partners, but that had been several years ago. Was he seeing anyone? Even when they'd been stressed from lack of sleep and an impending presentation deadline, he'd always been so *normal.* No weird issues. No disgusting habits. Definite marriage material. Some woman should have snapped him up by now. Cammy, herself, might have snapped him up if they hadn't been partners. And now that they weren't, well, there was Jonathan. Jonathan who made her feel alive and witty and talented. Jonathan who needed her and depended on her. Jonathan who mentored her. And someday, Jonathan was going to realize he loved her.

Gil was a great guy, but he'd done just fine without her. He'd mentioned a house, but not whether anyone was living in it with him. She should keep him in mind the next time one of her girlfriends complained that all the good men were taken. Assuming that he *wasn't* taken.

"It's been a long day and you're wet and hungry." He slipped his glasses back on. "I can't do anything about the first two, but I can feed you lasagna and a glass of red wine at Sorelli's."

Her absolute favorite comfort/celebration/indulgent/reward food at her absolute favorite restaurant. Cammy's stomach growled. She hoped the sound of the rain covered it up. "That sounds heavenly."

"Great. Let's go." And he was out of her car before she really decided to accept.

Oh, why not? Grabbing her purse, she followed him

But when she sat, drenched and dripping in Gil's car, Sorelli's didn't seem like such a good idea. Flipping her hair behind her shoulders, she pointed out the obvious, "We're all wet."

His gaze flicked over her. "Don't worry about it." He drove into the garage and began the downward spiral to the exit. "We'll sit in one of the back booths."

Cammy didn't remind him that it was a Friday night and the over-the-top, romantically decorated booths located in the odd nook left over from Sorelli's kitchen renovations were always reserved weeks in advance.

She knew because she'd reserved them for Jonathan many times.

Gil drove to the street level and swung into Jonathan's empty parking place right by the elevators.

So he'd left already, Cammy thought. She almost objected to Gil parking in Jonathan's place, but the entire level was deserted and Jonathan's slot *was* the nearest to the elevators. It made sense.

They descended to the tunnel system that ran beneath Houston's downtown. The place was like a mall and crowded with people who had decided to shop or eat dinner before beginning the wet commute home.

Cammy caught sight of herself in a store window and winced at her stringy hair. She'd been trying to grow it longer, but it didn't like longer. It liked above the shoulders. Beside her Gil watched as she fluffed her wet bangs.

Lucky man. He'd slicked back his hair once in the car, and then ignored it, revealing a high forehead she'd never noticed before. It made him look a lot more sophisticated and cerebral than the Gil she was used to seeing.

"Stop worrying about your hair," he told her. "This evening isn't going to be a good hair night for anybody."

Great. So it did look as bad as she thought.

Gil led her to the escalators that deposited them in the public lobby of the office tower next door to the restaurant. At the exit, he took her hand as they ran the few steps in the open before they ducked beneath Sorelli's green awning.

Other than the occasional high-five when something went well, Cammy didn't remember ever touching Gil before. His hand felt warm and strong and, to be honest, she was disappointed when he let go. She had to admit she liked his matter-of-fact confidence in shepherding her through the tunnels to Sorelli's welcoming foyer. Not that she needed shepherding. But it felt nice to be taken care of by a man for a change.

She missed that feeling. It had been a while since she'd had a boyfriend. She'd hoped that she and Jonathan...well.

Cammy swept her gaze over Gil as he spoke with the hostess, admiring how the parts of his body she'd noticed separately came together to form one very attractive man. Wait a minute. This was Gil. She blinked. Had he always looked like this? Really, wet clothes and slicked back hair shouldn't have made *that* much of difference.

Yes, it *had* been a long time between boyfriends.

He grinned at the hostess and Cammy became suddenly aware that while wet clothes made Gil appear appealingly disheveled, she just looked sad and messy.

She pointed to the ladies' room. "I'm going in there."

Once inside, she used rolled hand towels from the basket by the sink to blot at herself and her hair. Just as she thought, it was kinking its way up to her shoulders. She tucked her hair behind her ears and sighed. Drowned rat was not a good look for her.

She also touched up her makeup. If her hair was going to look bad, at least her face could look good.

Why do you care? It's just Gil.

Yeah, but Gil was looking mighty fine. Cammy saw the way the hostess had smiled at him after barely glancing at her. She saw the way he'd returned the smile, too.

She felt a little tickle of awareness when she thought about that smile. He'd never smiled at *her* that way.

Oh, good grief. Why would he? And why was she even thinking about this?

When she emerged, the hostess led her through a surprisingly empty restaurant to where Gil was waiting in one of the coveted back booths, a glass of red wine already in front of her place.

Cammy gracelessly slid her wet slacks across the velvet

seat. At least they were black in case the red dye in the velvet wasn't colorfast. She raised her wineglass to Gil. "My hero."

GIL'S HEART GAVE AN annoying blip. How many times had he imagined a rescue scenario like this? Well, here it was. His heart's desire.

Ya think?

It was a nothing remark; she'd been frustrated. Completely understandable given the circumstances. And she'd apologized. But she wouldn't have snapped at Jonathan and Gil couldn't get past that.

Ya think?

It was nothing, yet it was everything.

Cammy took a sip of wine and her eyebrows lifted. "This is good."

"I remember that you drink cabs," he said, "but Sorelli's is trying out a new house red and want our feedback. If you don't like it, they'll bring you something else."

She took another sip. "I do like it. But it wasn't what I was expecting. What is it?"

"A cab-shiraz-merlot blend." He watched her drink more. He'd planned to order her favorite cabernet just as he'd planned to order the lasagna. If he surrounded her with her favorite things, she'd feel happy and then she'd associate happy feelings with him—that was Gil's plan.

Ya think?

He'd ordered the blend instead.

It wasn't a good sign that he was rebelling against his own plan. The wine choice seemed to be a success, though, since Cammy had already drained half the over-size glass.

When the waiter brought their menus, Cammy waved them away. "I know what I want. The lasagna."

Gil wanted to order something different, but Sorelli's lasagna was killer and he hadn't eaten here in a couple of months. "I'll have the lasagna, as well, and a house salad," he told their server.

"Two lasagnas and two house salads," repeated the waiter.

"No salad for me," Cammy said. "I've had enough cold, wet things today. I'm going directly for the hot carbs."

Taking the hint, the waiter returned with an overloaded bread basket. As Cammy dived in, he started to ask if he could bring her another glass of wine, but Gil silently signaled him to bring the bottle.

While Cammy dipped foccacia in herbed olive oil, the waiter refilled her glass and set the bottle on the table.

"We're not going to need the whole bottle," she protested.

Gil moved it to the side. "We might be here a while." If all went well.

"True. And if we're going to be stuck somewhere, this is the place to be." Cammy sighed happily as she looked around at the naked cherubs cavorting amid hearts and flowers and birds. "I'm glad you got a booth. They must have had cancellations because of the weather."

"Yes." To Gil, it looked as though Valentine's Day had thrown up in the booth.

When he'd imagined his scenarios with Cammy, he'd neglected to imagine what they'd talk about or that there would be so many cherubs. Until this moment, conversation hadn't been an issue since Cammy's mouth had been filled with bread or wine. This was Gil's shot to make her aware of him as a man. It was time to say something and he knew what he didn't want to talk about, or rather who—Jonathan.

Think happy. Think witty. Think amusing. Think fun. Not that there was any pressure. "The last time I was here with you we were celebrating your birthday." Not a bad opener.

Cammy looked thoughtful as she tore more bread. "I

don't... Oh, when we were partners! I remember. That was a long time ago."

"Three years."

"It seems like forever."

"Yes." Where was the amusing wit?

"You and Paul are doing really well," she said.

"It's not the same magic you and I had, but it's pretty good."

Rolling her eyes, she said, "You are too kind."

"Not kind. It's the truth." He sipped at his wine.

"Not really." She shook her head. "Most of the ideas we developed were yours. And you were so much better at writing copy and I'm not that great at drawing. It's like, 'what was I thinking?' Why did I think I could make it in advertising?"

Who had convinced her she was no good? Gil had his suspicions. "Cammy, your ideas inspired other ideas. I remember you as an idea fountain. You were the spark that lit the fire. The gas that fueled the engine. The rain that made the desert bloom."

"Oh, come on!" She laughed. "You always were a sweetie."

A sweetie. She thought he was *sweet*. He was not sweet. He was patient, the way a lion patiently waits in the shadows for the ideal moment to capture his prey.

"That's why I enjoy working with Jonathan," she went on. "I'm learning so much."

Sometimes a lion has to steal prey from another predator. "And how are you using what you've learned?"

She stopped dipping bread long enough to glance at him. "What do you mean?"

He meant exactly what she suspected, that she was wasting her time, but he answered, "Are you analyzing data or looking to get back into the creative side, or what?"

"No—I brainstorm with Jonathan, though. And he's

always very good about listening and then showing me how my ideas miss the mark or how they can be improved."

Gil carefully set down his glass before he snapped the stem. "That's very generous of him." Gil didn't know whether he was angrier at Jonathan for using Cammy's ideas or for making her doubt her talent.

"Stop looking at me like that."

So much for fun and happiness. "Like what?" Gil's salad arrived so he looked at it instead.

"As though Jonathan is stealing my ideas."

"Is he?"

"No!" Cammy took a largish swallow of wine. "I'm brainstorming with him the same way we used to brainstorm. Ideas grow from other ideas. You know that."

"Mmm hmm." Gil topped off her glass.

"You can't single out a part of an idea and lay claim to it." She ripped off a hunk of bread. "Once it's out there, it's out there."

Gil ate his salad.

"And an idea is just an idea until it's developed. Jonathan is genius at making ideas workable."

"Yeah, he knows a good idea when he sees one." *Think about where he gets those ideas, Cammy.*

Oblivious, Cammy nodded and tried to drink wine at the same time. A drop or two escaped and she blotted her mouth with her napkin. Gil refreshed her glass.

"Besides, Jonathan gives me credit."

"Does he?" Gil asked mildly.

"When he lists the people assigned to the account, he'll put 'account assistant Cammy Philips' right there on the page."

Gil was having trouble swallowing. Apparently Cammy would swallow anything. "That's great," he said with forced cheer. "So you get to share in the KTSO pool."

She stopped in the act of bringing her glass to her mouth. "I… What are you talking about?"

Careful. Careful. "The bonus money. When the clients like the proposed campaign so much they increase their original advertising budget, the account team gets a percentage as a bonus," Gil explained. Cammy's arrested expression confirmed his suspicions that Jonathan hadn't spread the wealth. To be fair, he wasn't obligated to. Cammy was his assistant, not part of the creative team. "We call it KTSO money."

She sipped her wine thoughtfully.

Her cheeks were flushed and her hair had gone all fluffy and curly as it dried. Gil liked it that way, but knew she didn't. At least she hadn't straightened it and dyed it dark brown for Jonathan, although she'd stopped adding blond highlights.

Gil had always liked the way she looked. She was an under-the-radar girl. Appealing and approachable. A nice girl with stealth good looks. Totally underappreciated until one day something about her expression, or the way the light hits her face, or the way her hair gleams catches a guy's attention and he thinks, "Hey, she's really pretty." And then he falls for her and she becomes stunningly beautiful and the women who were getting all the attention before now look too obvious.

Or at least that's the way it had been for Gil.

Cammy focused her gaze on him. "What does KTSO mean?"

"Knock their socks off. A presentation so good it knocks the client's socks off."

She nodded slowly. "That's why Jonathan gave Ross those awful green socks he wears to presentations."

"Yeah. They're his lucky socks."

Gil wanted Cammy to think about the bonus money she

hadn't been getting, but their lasagna arrived and distracted her.

"Now *this* is the way to wait out a storm." She gave Gil a wide smile.

She looked so happy and soft and fuzzy and pink-cheeked that Gil wanted to wrap his arms around her and never let her go. He forgave her for being hung up on Jonathan because he was hung up on her.

But that didn't mean he enjoyed listening to her talk about the guy for the rest of the evening.

3

THE NEXT MORNING DID not begin well. In the first place, there wasn't a whole lot of morning left when Cammy woke up. In the rest of the places, she was incredibly thirsty, reeked of garlic and had fallen asleep in her underwear and top from yesterday.

And in a place all by itself, somebody was knocking at her door. Cammy got out of bed, stepping directly onto the still-damp slacks pooled on the floor.

More knocking. It wasn't pounding, not yet, but it sounded as if the insistent knocking wasn't going to stop, either.

She bent over to pick up her slacks. Mistake. Her head protested and her eyes felt funny.

When she flipped on the bathroom light she saw that she hadn't taken off her make up last night and the industrial-strength waterproof mascara she wore to withstand Houston's steamy summers had bent her eyelashes. But, by golly, it had not smeared.

Her hair was kinky poofed on one side and kinky flattened on the side of her head that she'd slept on. Her bangs stuck out.

And someone was still at her door.

Cammy gathered her hair into a ponytail, threw on some shorts and went to deal with the knocking.

Her keys hung from the lock. She never left her keys there. As she reached for them, a memory surfaced. She was standing here, yawning, trying to turn the key and a voice outside the door was telling her to turn it the other direction.

Gil's voice.

And her voice saying, "You're a really nice guy, you know that?"

And he saying, "I know. You've told me. Turn the key until it clicks."

She *had* told him he was a nice guy. Many times. For taking her to dinner. For driving her home. For helping her up the stairs. She cringed. She'd clung pretty tightly as he'd helped her up the stairs, not because she couldn't walk up them by herself, but because she'd discovered the lovely muscles in his arms.

Which she'd also told him about.

And then…no. No. She did *not* pucker up for a goodnight kiss. But, in contrast with the fuzzy memories, there was this horribly clear one of Cammy swaying unsteadily toward Gil's mouth and missing and landing near his nose. She remembered his hands on her shoulders as he gently, but insistently, disentangled himself, since she'd made another attempt to kiss him and had looped her arms around his neck to improve her aim.

Cammy closed her eyes and touched her forehead to the front door, jumping when whoever was on the other side knocked again.

She had an idea who it was.

"Cammy?"

Yep. Gil.

What had she been thinking? She remembered talking and talking and waving garlic bread all around at dinner and feeling witty, and smart, and warm….

And a wineglass that was always full.

She yanked open the door. "You got me drunk!"

Gil's gaze swept over her and zeroed in on her eyes, especially the left one she was having trouble blinking. "You insisted you were just pleasantly buzzed."

"I don't feel pleasant."

"You don't look pleasant." He, on the other hand, looked new-morning fresh in a black T-shirt with some grunge logo on it and cargo shorts as he walked past her and headed toward her kitchen. A black T-shirt? When had Gil become a black rock-band T-shirt kind of guy? With broad shoulders? And nice abs?

"Wait a minute!" She shut the door and trailed after him.

Gil opened and closed her kitchen cabinets until he found a glass, which he filled with water and carried into her bedroom.

"Hey!" she protested before following him like a puppy.

He was in her bathroom, looking in the medicine cabinet.

When she appeared in the doorway, he handed her the glass, opened a bottle of aspirin and shook out two. "Take these."

Cammy straightened. "I am not—"

Gil popped the aspirin in her mouth. They tasted so bad that Cammy swallowed some water.

"Drink it all."

Giving in was easier than arguing with him.

He took the empty glass and gestured for her to precede him out of the bathroom. Then he picked up her slacks and draped them over a towel rack.

"I was getting to that," she muttered.

He ignored her.

She couldn't tell if he was angry or trying not to laugh or was totally disgusted with her.

"What are you doing here?" she asked.

"You don't have a car, remember?"

"Of course I remember," she snapped and then modified her tone. "But you could have called first."

"I did. Repeatedly."

He was back in the kitchen and, oh please let it be, putting a Starbucks cup in her microwave. How had she missed the cup on the counter? It was for her, wasn't it? Wasn't it?

"I guess I didn't hear my phone." Her purse was here on the kitchen bar. She dug through it looking for her phone. Not there. Had she lost her phone last night?

Just as the microwave dinged, Cammy remembered getting ready to call AAA for roadside assistance. Then Gil had pulled up beside her…. "I must have left my phone in my car."

"That explains why you didn't answer."

This was bad. Very bad. What if Jonathan had needed her?

Gil swirled the coffee cup to redistribute any hot spots, and set it in front of her. "Latte."

"Thank you." She was pathetically grateful. "You're very sweet."

"So you've said." He sounded a little frosty.

Cammy took a restorative swallow of coffee. "I did, didn't I?" When she hadn't been telling him he was nice, she'd been telling him he was sweet. She stared at the coffee lid. "I take it you don't like being called sweet."

"Little girls in pink dresses are sweet. Kittens are sweet. Grandmothers' kisses are sweet. The deal I got on my sound system was sweet."

"Okay. You're not sweet."

"No, I'm not."

Surprised at his tone, she glanced up and blinked.

Something about him was different. "You're not wearing your glasses."

"I'm going back to contacts."

"And you haven't been wearing glasses since you got here?"

He gave her a half smile that had no business being sexy but was. "No."

Cammy made an exasperated sound. "How much wine did I drink last night?"

"Most of the bottle."

"No way!" She narrowed her eyes, feeling her stiff, crooked lashes stab her lids. "I never have more than two glasses!"

"We were there over three hours. You also ate two baskets of bread."

And still reeked of garlic, he didn't say.

There was a lot he wasn't saying. She could see his jaw tense with the effort of holding it back, too. He looked… stern. Detached. And whatever opinion of her he was hiding behind his professionally blank gaze was not good.

And why would it be? She'd been a drunken pig. A garrulous, drunken pig. She'd monopolized the conversation talking on and on about all the wonderful things Jonathan had taught her. Priceless things. Invaluable nuggets of information it would have taken her years to learn on her own. Knowledge was worth a lot more than any sock money.

That was the point she'd been trying to make to Gil, but was aware she wasn't selling it. As he'd sat across the booth from her, she'd wanted to see the expression on his face change from skepticism to understanding with a touch of envy. Make that a moderate envy.

There was no envy now. He glanced down at the wrinkled blouse she'd slept in. "The rain has mostly stopped. Go shower and we'll get your car."

So she was a drunken, garrulous, *smelly* pig. Lovely.

The drive to the parking garage was silent. Gil wasn't normally talkative, but this silence was uncomfortable. There was more to it than Cammy drinking a little too much wine and hogging the bread basket and kissing him goodnight. Or trying to.

Maybe he was just annoyed that he had to give up part of his Saturday to take her back to her car. Maybe he had plans. Cammy found herself wondering what plans Gil might have. Obviously, he had a life outside Peck and Davilla, but she knew nothing about it.

The day was cloudy and the wind had died down by the time Gil parked nose-to-nose with her car on the parking-garage roof.

Cammy could hardly wait to get out of his car. Opening the door to hers, she saw her cell phone on the seat. She held it up. "At least I didn't lose my phone." As Gil walked over to stand next to her, she checked for messages. "Wow. You did call a bunch."

"I wanted to be sure you were okay."

"Thanks," she said absently as she scrolled through the list of missed calls and texts. "There are tons of messages. Something must be going on." She started reading.

Cammy, what's up with Jonathan and the beach house?

I can't reach Jonathan, is he still going to the beach house?

Jonathan's mailbox is full. Tell him I'm not going to make it.

She looked up at Gil. "People are asking me about the beach house. Jonathan's using it this weekend. I guess he's throwing a party."

Cammy felt a pang. How many people had he invited? And when was he going to invite her to one of his parties?

She read the text Jonathan had sent right after she'd told him the beach house was available. And suddenly, there it was at last—her invitation. She beamed up at Gil, smiling so wide she felt it in her cheeks. "Jonthan's throwing a party and he asked me! I'm supposed to bring the steaks and breakfast."

LOOK AT HER FACE, Gil ordered himself. Cammy was glowing and twinkling and radiating happiness. Because of Jonathan. Because Jonathan had finally noticed her in the way she'd wanted him to notice her. *Memorize her expression and think of it every time you want to pass up the chance to be with another woman in case Cammy's available.*

Cammy Philips would never be his. She would never look at him as though he lit up her whole world, no matter how much he wanted her to. Her drunken attempt at a kiss last night meant nothing. She probably didn't remember.

But Gil remembered. He remembered how her body had felt against his as he'd walked her up the stairs. He remembered that one moment when she'd stood outside her door and looked at him and something had changed in her eyes. In that instant, she'd forgotten about Jonathan and had finally become aware of Gil as a man. When she'd tilted her head up, his heart had pounded because he was going to kiss her at last. But then she'd wobbled and his heart had slowed. He hadn't wanted her to kiss him because she'd drunk too much wine. He wanted her to choose him. Choose him over Jonathan.

And that would never happen. So from now on, he was also going to dress the way he wanted, cut his hair and wear his contacts. If molding himself into Cammy's ideal man hadn't worked by now, it was never going to.

"No wonder Jonathan was surprised to see me after the

meeting," Cammy was saying. "He told me to go on and he'd see me later—he meant last night! I was supposed to meet him there last night." She looked stricken. "I'm calling him." She hit the speed dial. After several moments during which Gil tortured himself by remembering her ecstatic expression, she closed her phone. "His voice mail is still full. Something must have happened to him!"

"Nothing happened to him." Gil should be so lucky.

"I've got to get to the beach house!" She was talking in exclamation points now.

"See if your car will start first."

Cammy sat and jabbed her key into the ignition. Gil stood by the open door and felt a little sick at the way her hands shook with excitement.

No. He had no chance with her.

The car clicked. Cammy stared in disbelief. "I thought it would start once the rain quit. Do you think it's still wet? This hasn't happened before."

"Pop the hood, and I'll take a look," Gil told her.

Cammy released the latch. "Do you know much about cars?"

"No," he answered from beneath the hood. "But I know that when water and electricity get together they do bad things to wiring. Come see."

Cammy joined him and Gil pointed to some wires with bits of rust and corrosion on them. "Looks like something arced when moisture got to it." He had no idea if that was true, but he'd heard a guy say it once and it sounded impressive. Besides, the bottom line was that her car wouldn't start and he didn't know how to fix it. He shut the hood.

"But what about Jonathan's party?"

Gil shook his head. "Sorry."

She clutched his arm. "You don't understand, there are people there and Jonathan is depending on me to bring food!"

"Cammy, they're not going to starve."

"But what if something bad happened? He's not answering his phone!"

"Maybe he's sleeping in." *With a woman who is not you.*

"Or maybe the house collapsed in the storm and he's lying unconscious in the wreckage!"

"We would have heard."

"How?"

Her fingers hurt his arm. Gil peeled them off and looked into her hysteria-tinged eyes. He was going to regret his next words. "Okay, I'll drive you to the beach house."

Hope flared in her expression. "Gil, I can't ask—"

"I'm offering."

Unbelievably, she hesitated. "I…I don't want Jonathan to think… I mean, when he sees us together…" she trailed off.

And Gil understood. His heart might have even turned to lead right then. "Don't worry. I won't let him get the wrong idea about us. I'll make sure he knows you're available in every way."

4

HOURS AND HOURS AND hours—Gil couldn't believe how many hours—later he and Cammy were stuck in a line of cars headed toward the coast. This was after they'd driven all over Houston for supplies Cammy thought she should take to the beach house. Supplies such as bottled water and candles and charcoal and batteries and canned food and all the popular items that people had already cleaned off store shelves like locusts attacking a field of corn.

It was torture watching her frantic preparations, but seeing her going crazy over Jonathan was a necessary step in his getting-over-Cammy process.

Next to him, Cammy fidgeted and fretted about the time. "I should be there. I always organize these events, so it's not going to occur to Jonathan to bring water and ice and food."

It was like watching a train wreck. He couldn't look away. "Cammy, Jonathan and his party pals can always get back in their cars and drive home."

"But it's my job to take care of the details! I was supposed to be there last night and I wasn't. Jonathan's going to look bad and it will be my fault."

"What's he going to do, fire you?"

She gasped.

Oh, hell. "He's not going to fire you. Trust me on this." Gil stared at the long line of slow-moving cars in front of them. "The party sounds like a casual spur-of-the-moment thing, not like an official company event you were supposed to arrange."

"Then why did he invite company employees?" She exhaled and tried calling Jonathan again.

Gil figured she'd called him about fifty times already.

She snapped her phone closed. "Why is there so much traffic?"

"It's a Saturday. People are returning home and beach-house owners are checking on their property. There could be road damage or flooding or the county officials might not be letting people into the area." Gil kept his voice calm to hide his irritation. He wanted to stay irritated. It kept him from pulling off the road and grabbing her, first to shake sense into her and then to kiss sense into her. He'd probably skip the shaking and just go for the kissing. In spite of everything he wanted to kiss her. Just once. Okay, more than once, but at least once because he never had. He needed closure.

Forget closure. He just wanted to kiss her. He kept thinking about the feel of her lips next to his nose last night and didn't want that to be his only kissing memory.

If he still wanted her after listening to her go on about Jonathan, how was he ever going to stop wanting her? Because he did, in spite of her tunnel vision and her fidgeting and her infatuation with the ultimate player.

He was as hopeless as she was.

She moaned and rubbed her temples with both hands.

"Headache?"

Cammy dropped her hands. "Yes."

"Then let's just forget going to the beach house and drive back home."

"No!" She glared at him. "Why would I want to do that?"

"Oh, I don't know." His fingers tapped against the steering wheel. "Maybe because you don't even know if he's there?"

"He's there." She sounded utterly sure. "And he's probably worried that I haven't shown up."

"Then why hasn't he called you?"

It was a reasonable question, but Cammy didn't answer. Instead, she opened her phone and hit Redial. Gil could hear when the call went straight to the mailbox-full message.

"Cammy, he's not worth this," he said quietly.

"Yes, he *is!*"

"Why?" He wanted her to admit that she was in love with Jonathan—to hear her say it. Maybe that would break the hold she had over him.

"Because he's our extremely talented and successful Creative Director. Technically, he's your boss, too. Why wouldn't you do everything you could to support him?"

Gil let her question hang in the air and then decided to answer. "Because I'm not in love with him and you are."

CAMMY LITERALLY STOPPED breathing. Was that a lucky guess or did Gil know? After a couple of beats went by, she managed a credible laugh. "Because I care about doing a good job? Oh, please."

"It's way more than a job to you," Gil went on. "It's your excuse to stay close to him. You're obsessed with the guy and everyone knows it. Including Jonathan."

People knew? *Everyone* knew? Jonathan knew? She was going to be sick. Swallowing hard, she tried damage control. "I can't believe you said that." Her heart raced. "I can't believe our work ethic has deteriorated to the extent that when someone works hard and does her job to the very best of her ability, people think something's wrong or that she's 'obsessed.'" She glared at him. "Look at that. I'm so upset I used finger quotes."

He held her gaze. "You're in love with Jonathan Black. No finger quotes. Admit it."

"I am not."

Gil looked forward as the traffic moved a few feet. "You broke up our team and took an intern-level position that you've clung to for three years during which you've become Jonathan Black's personal servant." He threw her a glance before checking the rearview mirror. "You're nothing but a flunky in a low-paid, dead-end job."

Her chest hurt. How dare he say these things to her? "I get it. You're just mad because I didn't want to be your partner anymore."

"I'm disgusted because you threw away your career so you could hang around in case he noticed you. Not gonna happen."

If Gil had been shouting or angry at her, his words wouldn't have cut as deeply as this dispassionate recital.

"He's my mentor. I took the opportunity to learn from the best." She could hardly hear her voice over the pulsing in her ears.

But she heard his.

"You think if you make yourself indispensible that one day, he'll blink and say, 'Why Cammy, you're beautiful. I've been so blind! Let's have sex.'"

She gasped. *"I do not."*

"But if he did say that, you'd do it, wouldn't you? Right in his office. You take care of everything else in his life, why not that, too?"

Cammy's hands shook. She had to get away from Gil. She had to get away from the awful things he was saying. "Stop the car."

"It's not moving that fast. If you want to go for a dramatic jump from a moving vehicle, now's your chance. You probably won't break anything."

She stared at Gil. Never in a million years would she have imagined this conversation with him. "I hate you."

"Good." He nodded to himself. "That's good."

"Why?"

"Because now maybe you'll wake up to the fact that there's no hope, no chance, no way Jonathan will ever love you." Gil faced her full-on. "He's using you and he'll keep using you as long as a little flirting will keep you hanging in there."

"You can't— You don't..." Her chest was so tight she couldn't get enough air. "I want out of this car." Her voice quivered and Cammy honestly didn't know if it was from shock, anger—or the fact that he might be right. She grabbed the door handle, but it was locked. "Let me out!" She pulled on the lock, but Gil overrode it from his side. "Unlock the door!"

He ran his hands through his hair and gripped the steering wheel. "Cammy—"

"Now!"

Abruptly, and totally illegally, Gil pulled into the emergency lane and passed the line of stalled cars until he exited the highway. They were out in the middle of nowhere. The intersection at the underpass was nothing but a four-way stop with a combination gas station and bait shop a few hundred yards down the road to the right. Undeveloped flat land with tall spindly grass and billboards surrounded them.

Cammy pointed a shaking finger. "Pull in to the bait shop."

"It's closed."

"I don't care!"

Gil drove to the entrance. A hand-lettered sign on the door read Power Out.

"Now what?" he asked.

Cammy gathered her purse. “Drive around back.”

Gil circled past the gas pumps and stopped. No cars were parked by the back entrance. Cammy had hoped someone might be inside so she could pay them to drive her to the beach house. No matter. She’d think of something. “Let me out.” She wanted to get as far away from Gil as she could.

Yanking on the handle, she was surprised when it gave and she nearly fell out. Slamming the door behind her, she marched toward the empty boxes by the trash, intending to sit on one and call her friends until she found someone who would come and rescue her from the horrible Gil. But as soon as she saw the boxes, she remembered the supplies in the back of his SUV and turned around.

He was leaning against his car, arms crossed over his chest, watching her. Something about the way the late-afternoon light burnished his skin or the expression on his face or the way his brown eyes focused on her said “man.” Shouted “man,” actually.

A whisper of awareness bubbled through her. *This is Gil.* Gil. *You hate him, remember? His bad-boy pose is just to show off his chest and arms. So what if they’re worth showing off? You still hate him.*

The air outside the car was hot and sticky and a rotten fish smell hung over the trash cans. No way could she stay there.

Cammy walked back to the car acutely aware of Gil watching her every move. Now that he no longer wore glasses, his brown eyes appeared more intense. If she didn’t hate him, she might use the word *smoldering* to describe them. So let him smolder. She was angry, too.

As Cammy drew closer, Gil swept his gaze over her. She wore a white tank top and pale blue denim shorts. Perfectly respectable. Except that the way Gil was looking at her didn’t make her feel very respectable.

A male work colleague should not look at a female work

colleague as though he was imagining her naked. Completely inappropriate.

To her mortification, Cammy felt her body respond with gathering warmth in the places where his eyes lingered. Her skin felt tingly and tight.

When she realized she was breathing through her mouth, she brought her lips together and swallowed. Gil's mouth curved in a knowing smirk. Cammy felt a rush of desire so strong she stumbled. To cover, she bent and pretended to take a piece of crushed shell out of her sandal. She straightened and caught Gil's gaze lingering where her neckline gapped. He wasn't smoldering with anger, he was just smoldering. And doing it very well. So well, that Cammy almost forgot that she hated him.

"Change your mind?" he asked when she reached him.

When had his voice deepened?

Ignoring the way it vibrated through her, she continued to the back of the car. "I forgot the supplies and food." She opened the cargo door.

Gil closed it. "I'm not going to leave you here alone."

He sounded very manly and mature and she was throwing a tantrum. So not like her. But she wasn't feeling like herself, either. She felt anxious, unsettled, and she stood way too close to him, so close she started noticing things like the arch of his eyebrows and the tiny curl of hair that touched one of his earlobes. She caught the steady up-and-down movement of his shoulders as he breathed. And she wanted to lick the place where his neck met his shoulder. To be honest, she'd happily lick a lot more.

Her skin prickled because she wanted him to touch her. The *exact* places she wanted to be touched were throbbing. Where had this reaction come from?

Okay. Enough. Between her car, the worry about the beach-house party, the anger over Gil's words and the fear that everyone at work knew her secret, she was on emotional overload, that's all.

"C'mon." He gestured with his head.

She didn't have a lot of options, but that didn't mean she'd just meekly get back into the car. "Not until you apologize for the things you said." She tilted her chin up to show she was serious.

Drawing his hands to his waist, he stared down at her and she had no idea what he was thinking. He wasn't apologizing, she knew that.

Gil blinked once and the rest happened in slow motion. He stepped closer and Cammy felt the heat of his body even in the warm, sticky air. She caught his scent over the smelly garbage. His head tilted and the hair on her arms tickled as his hands brushed past on their way to cupping her face. Her heart thundered, sensing before her brain that he was going to kiss her. Her lips parted in a gasp as he bent his head and took her mouth in a full-on kiss.

That first touch was like a jolt of static electricity and she gasped again, inhaling his breath. He leaned into the kiss, fitting her mouth to his, and then settled in to create some serious sizzle.

A roaring filled her ears as her heart went crazy and everything in her started shouting "Yes!" Her brain was short-circuiting and her blood had gone fizzy. All the ambiguous restlessness she'd felt earlier had become desire and that desire was focused on her mouth, which was attached to Gil's mouth.

Gil. Out of nowhere, she'd discovered this incredible chemistry with Gil. Cammy was having a tough time with the concept, so she just went with it, relaxing and pressing her body against his surprisingly lumpy one—and not the good kind of lump. And then she realized she still had a grip on her purse between them and dropped it. Winding her arms around his neck, she relaxed into him. It was a lot better now that there was just the one lump.

Without breaking their kiss, Gil released her face and splayed one hand over her back and one hand on her bottom.

And squeezed.

Cammy gave a yelp of surprise which opened her mouth wider. Gil plunged his tongue inside and pressed her into the cradle of his thighs at the same time.

Melting. She was melting. All the sizzling and the fizzing and the short circuiting was going to dissolve her into a warm little bubbling puddle right at Gil's feet. Either this was the best kiss of her life or it had been so long since she'd been kissed, she'd forgotten how good it could be. Probably both.

Being wrapped in his arms felt shockingly right, awakening a need and filling it at the same time.

And he tasted great. She probably tasted like garlic. He didn't seem to mind.

He moved his fingers lightly across the strip of skin above her waistband but mostly, he concentrated on the kiss and using his tongue to stroke and sensitize.

She was lost in time, oblivious to everything but the sensations Gil aroused in her. When he began to pull back, Cammy embarrassed herself by letting a whimper of protest escape before she could stop it.

Gil softened the kiss, lingering a little longer, nuzzling her lips before lifting his head. It was a total contrast to the sudden full throttle beginning and devastatingly effective.

Oh. So that's what a kiss is supposed to be like. Good to know.

Gill gazed down at her, his arms still holding her. Of course her arms were around his neck, so he could hardly go anywhere. And from the waist down, she might as well have been glued to him.

Dazed, she gradually became aware of her surroundings as one by one her senses focused outward again. She heard the distant rumble of traffic from the highway, felt a trickle of sweat run between her shoulder blades and noticed the decaying fish smell of the garbage. And in front of her stood Gil. Gil, who had just kissed her senseless. Gil whom she hated. She tried to remember why she hated Gil.

Because he'd accused her of loving Jonathan, which she'd denied…and then he'd kissed her and she…had possibly kissed him back with an enthusiasm that proved she *didn't* love Jonathan.

She hated him for doing that to her. Abruptly pushing herself out of his arms, Cammy gathered the remnants of her earlier anger. "What kind of apology was that?"

He grinned, looking pleased with himself. "One you liked."

It was hard to maintain a self-righteous anger while parts of her body still throbbed with pleasure from the best kiss she'd had in her entire life. "You're very technically adept."

"You're very hot."

Not nearly as hot as the look he gave her. Cammy could feel her skin tingling again. This time, she recognized it as desire for his touch. The only relief she'd found had been when he was holding her. Even now, the skin near the small of her back prickled because his fingers had caressed her there.

This was awful. She wasn't supposed to be attracted to Gil. Attracted. Ha. He'd unleashed a raging lust. Cammy wasn't a lustful person, yet she could barely look at him without panting in desire. She wanted to rip off his shirt and feel his skin. She wanted to rip off *her* shirt and rub against him.

She hated feeling so aware of him, as though all her nerves were standing on tiptoe in order to get closer to him.

Lust seemed like such a simple emotion. Maybe that's why it was so strong.

Cammy stepped back and dragged in a lungful of air to ease the tightness in her chest. She figured she'd have to live with the throbbing.

Gil bent down and picked up her purse.

"Why?" She took it from him. "Why did you kiss me?"

He gave her a lopsided smile. "Because I'm in love with you."

All the air she'd painfully worked into her lungs whooshed out. "You are not."

"Don't think I'm unaware of the irony. You stuck on Jonathan. Me stuck on you."

Cammy held her breath because she was dangerously close to hyperventilating. She did not need this. She knew what Gil was doing: this was a test. The kiss, his false declaration of love, all of it was a way to prove she didn't really love Jonathan. Which was what she wanted him to believe. Which he didn't.

"So what do you think is going to happen here? Am I supposed to look at you and say, 'Why, Gil, you're so handsome. I've been so blind. Let's have sex'?"

A smile indicated that he recognized his words to her earlier. "Works for me."

"Right here, right now?"

"Better and better."

One of them was going to blink first. It wasn't going to be Cammy. She yanked open the car door and tossed her purse into the cargo area. "How about the backseat?"

"That'd be great." Gil reached for a lever at the side of the bench seat and pushed at the back until it lay flat.

It looked like a bed. Cammy's anger faded as something that felt like panic but was probably excitement took over. She didn't want to analyze exactly what was going on here, but she wanted to win. "I suppose you've got a condom with you."

"No. But you've got some in your purse." Gil leaned over to dig in it as Cammy's mouth dropped open. How did he know? Embarrassment made her skin hot and then clammy as he triumphantly held up a string of three.

Defiantly, she snatched them out of his hand and tucked them into the space where the headrest met the seat back. "There. All ready. It's always awkward when the mood gets broken because the man has to stop and fumble for a condom."

"I never fumble."

"You've never had sex in the backseat of a car, either."

He just grinned.

Oh, hell. Now what?

"After you." Still grinning, he gestured to the car, calling her bluff.

He thought he had her. He thought she'd chicken out.

Facing him, Cammy crossed her arms, grabbed the hem of her tank top and pulled it off in one quick movement. "Not a lot of headroom in there. This way nobody takes an elbow to the face."

"I like the way you think." Gil pulled his shirt off one-handed revealing a sculpted torso to go along with the shoulders she'd noticed last night. Balling up his shirt, he threw it toward the front seat.

Cammy would have given anything to have been able to look him up and down in a casual I-suppose-you'll-do kind of way, but her eyes and already gone wide. "Gil!"

He looked down at himself. "I go to the company gym to think."

"You must think a lot."

"Yeah."

Gil wasn't body-builder beefy, but his slim, defined torso would draw eyes at any beach. They certainly drew hers.

Cammy didn't know how long she would have stood there and salivated, but a stray breeze twirled across the parking lot and the feel of it against skin that normally wasn't exposed reminded her that she was standing outside in her bra with a half-naked man.

All in all, she'd been worse places.

He hooked his thumbs in the waistband of his shorts and Cammy was half afraid, half hopeful that he would take them off. "Second thoughts?"

Glancing up, she saw the banked desire in his eyes. He'd already prepared himself for her to change her mind. "Just admiring the view."

With a lazy gesture, he reached for her shoulder and slipped his fingers beneath her bra strap. "If you expect me to back off because I'm nice or sweet, don't. Anything you offer, I'm taking. And I'll make you offer more." He tugged until the strap slowly whispered over her shoulder and then dragged his knuckles against the side of her breast.

Her nipples tightened. There would have been something wrong with her if they hadn't.

Okay, change of plan. Before she called a halt, since he obviously wasn't going to, Cammy would get him all hot and bothered. *Then* she'd stop. It was evil and wicked but she'd enjoy herself and make her point, too. A little voice asked exactly what her point was, but Cammy ignored it.

He thought he knew how this was going to play out. Cammy wanted to shake him up. Maybe she wanted to shake herself up, too. Reaching around to her back, she unhooked her bra and shimmied it off her arms. Tossing it over her shoulder in the general direction of the car, she said, "And I'll make you beg."

5

CAMMY ONLY GAVE HERSELF a couple of seconds to savor the stunned expression on Gil's face before she climbed into the car. Even though she barely recognized herself, she still wasn't an exhibitionist at heart.

Gil was in the car with the door closed and leaning toward her before she had time to crawl all the way over. "This is so much better than my fantasies about you."

Gil had fantasies? About her?

His eyes dark with desire, he skimmed his hands from her waist to her breasts. "Sooo much better."

Heat pooled in her belly with frightening speed. Her last thought before Gil's mouth closed over her nipple was that she'd be okay as long as she kept her shorts on.

His touch was all heat and sizzle and she felt it everywhere. There was no slow buildup, just an explosion of sensation. Her hips bucked as he teased her with his tongue. She felt one of his hands wander to the snap on her jean shorts. *Yes,* she thought, her brain clouded by lust, and then remembered *no.* Capturing his hand, she placed it on her other breast and then tunneled her fingers through his hair.

Pleasure rushed through her. Oh, he was good. Really good. She moaned. Really, really good. He knew just how to touch her and keep her suspended in the sweet spot between too much and not enough.

Normally, there wasn't such a thing as too good, but Cammy's plan was already in serious peril. She couldn't stop after a few breathless moans and *oh yes*es, not when she was writhing beneath him and practically pulling out his hair. It had been less than a minute and she was already rounding the corner at "Don't stop" and heading for "Hurry!" Nothing left after that but the slide into home.

Time to take it down a notch. She tugged on his shoulders. "Kiss me."

Gil shifted until his mouth was over hers. Instead of kissing her immediately, he slowly brushed stray pieces of her hair off her face. He wound one piece around his finger and let the curl spring loose. "I like your curly hair."

"It's a frizzy mess."

Gil shook his head. "You're beautiful." And then he did a rotten thing—he stared directly into her eyes and gave her the most tender smile. It pierced her heart, that smile. When he lowered his head and softly kissed her, she shivered, nearly overwhelmed with emotion.

She wasn't supposed to be feeling all gooshy about Gil, not when she hated him. But he'd looked at her with his heart in his eyes and she'd felt so mean about getting him all worked up and then stopping. Especially since she was all worked up and confused. She was supposed to be in love with Jonathan.

She closed her eyes and kissed Gil, pretending she was kissing Jonathan.

And felt nothing. Actually, she felt annoyed because Jonathan was intruding on her lovely kiss with Gil. Gil who had rescued her. Gil who had taken her to her favorite restaurant. Gil who had given up his Saturday to drive her to the beach house. Gil who had brought her coffee.

Gil who was making her feel so delicious.

Cammy ran her hands over his back and wrapped her leg around his waist. He felt so good against her, and warm, and solid, and he truly was the best kisser in the world. He gave her long, slow, syrupy kisses that tugged on her soul and deeper passionate kisses that heated her to the boiling point. The time to call a halt came and went and Cammy mentally waved good-bye to her plan. It was a stupid plan, anyway.

Reaching between their bodies, she tried to unsnap her shorts or his shorts or *somebody's* shorts but Gil's body was pressed so tightly against her she couldn't.

"Gil!" she cried in frustration. "Gil!"

HAVING CAMMY HALF-NAKED in his arms after so long was almost too good to be true. Gil poured everything he had into kissing and teasing and stroking and anything else he could think of to keep her squirming and making those sexy little sounds.

When she'd challenged him and tossed her bra over her shoulder, his caveman instincts had kicked in and he'd been fighting the urge to rip off the rest of her clothes and perpetuate the human race. He had more finesse than that.

He'd let her get into the car first.

Gil had gone from loving her in an idealistic way to enjoying her in a carnal way. He enjoyed her mouth and he enjoyed her breasts and he wanted to enjoy other places.

She was hot. She was panting. She was wiggling.

She was beating on his shoulders. "Gil!"

Her distressed voice finally penetrated. Gil dragged his mouth away from her and supported himself with his arms. Head hanging down, shoulders heaving, he softly groaned. He'd known it was too good to be true. She'd been mad at him and somehow that had translated into a heavy make-out session—he didn't follow the logic, but he sure wasn't complaining—but he'd known she'd have second thoughts.

"Gil, I—"

"It's okay, Cammy." He tried to keep the screaming sexual frustration out of his voice. "It's okay." He sucked in a huge breath of air, raised his head, and kissed her on the forehead murmuring, "It's okay."

"Gil—"

"It's okay."

Cammy groaned.

"I said I'd take everything you offered. That also means I'm not taking anything you don't."

"That's nice," she panted. "Help me get off my shorts."

He raised his head and blinked several times, mentally and physically doing a one-eighty. "I can do that."

He rolled to the side and helped Cammy draw off her shorts and underwear. And then he stared at her body concentrating fiercely so he'd remember every curve and every dimple and the way her skin glistened. He stared at the neat triangle at the juncture of her thighs, highlighted by the untanned skin, and thought, *this has been worth the wait.*

"Gil?" She nudged him with her foot.

"Hmm?"

"Take off your shorts."

"I can do that, too." He'd forgotten he still had them on.

"Good."

He scrambled out of them, sacrificing style for expediency.

He felt her hand run up and down his back and swallowed. He'd make this good for her if it killed him.

"It's time to get the condom," she said.

"Thank God."

"And can you turn around while you do that?"

Gil stopped in the act of reaching for the packet she'd propped in the headrest. "Turn around?"

"Yeah, so I can see."

He hadn't planned on making a big production out of it, but he turned around.

"It's a personal rule that nothing goes inside me without me seeing it first. It's also a personal rule not to have sex in the backseat of a car, but there you go." Cammy propped herself on her elbows and watched interestedly. "Now *that's* worth an exception to the rule, that is."

Gil fumbled with the condom.

"Ha! You said you never fumbled."

"You're staring! I feel like I'm auditioning. Talk about breaking the mood."

"Oh, please. Nothing's broken."

"Just my manly pride," he said darkly.

"Your manly pride is taking a quick breather before gearing up."

"That's not the way it's gearing." How could this be happening? With Cammy? With Cammy naked in his car? The thought alone should be plenty. The reality should have him like—

"Oh, Gi-il..."

He looked up, his gaze traveling up her legs, across the dewy expanse of her stomach, climbing over the peaks of her breasts, lingering in the hollow of her throat and hauling itself over her chin to meet her eyes.

When she had his attention, Cammy gently sucked on one finger, swirling her tongue around and around the tip before trailing it over her chin, between her breasts, and all the way down her stomach, retracing the path his gaze had just taken.

And then her knees fell open and she began touching herself.

The breath hissed between his teeth as lust exploded inside him. His heart pounded in his ears, his temples, his chest and his groin. He stared transfixed as her finger circled and dipped and rubbed.

"Don't think," she murmured. "Keep the blood flowing to the important parts."

"Okay," he said. "I can do that."

She smiled the most un-Cammylike smile he'd ever seen. "I'm going to stop giving stage directions now and let you slide on home."

"You're using sports metaphors?"

She settled back down, eyes closed. "If you can say 'metaphor,' you're thinking too much."

Right. Simple. Keep it simple. He knelt between her legs and caught Cammy's hand. Kissing it, he took her other hand and stretched them both over her head, pinning them against the seat.

Surprised, her eyes flew open and he grinned. *Yeah, you didn't expect that. Makes us even, because I didn't expect you.* Then he kissed her. Once, twice. She made the little sound he'd been waiting for. He kissed her a third time and her hips ground against his. He raised his lips, waiting, and only when her eyes opened again did he rock into her, not stopping until he was completely encased by her heat.

"Gil!" Her eyes were wide with shocked pleasure before growing heavy-lidded as a sensual smile curved her lips. "Is that all you've got?"

He thrust into her, setting a pace fueled by three years of longing and frustration.

Beneath him, Cammy moved her head from side to side and moaned as she tugged at her wrists. "Gil!"

He released them and she clutched his back and wrapped her legs around him.

Gil let go, pounding into her, claiming her for his own as she panted his name over and over. *His* name.

Her muscles clenched around him as she climaxed. He slowed, feeling a primal satisfaction as he felt the ripples and heard her moan his name. And then he said, "Cammy," and lost himself in her.

6

SHE HADN'T KEPT HER shorts on and now she was in trouble. Hot and sticky and naked in a car in a parking lot with no bathroom to duck into and stare at herself in the mirror and say, "What were you *thinking?*"

Cammy had been thinking of sex, that's what. The sex had been incredible. But it had been incredible with Gil.

What did that say about her? Probably something slutty because any sex that good had to be wrong somehow. It was like a life rule.

She didn't recognize herself. Sex in a semi-public place. In the daylight. And not with the man she'd been in love with for three years—or thought she'd been in love with for three years—but Gil.

She'd never acted this way before and wondered why. It was fun. She'd had a good time. People would be appalled. *She* would be appalled. But she felt smug.

The downside was that this situation wasn't real. It was some fluke, maybe due to low barometric pressure or something. It wasn't normal. And she was thinking *why can't it be normal?* which was the trouble part.

Beside her, Gil was talking. And talking.

She wasn't listening. Worse than that, she wanted him to

stop talking so they could have sex again. They were good at sex. She turned onto her side, propping herself on her elbow and watched Gil talk. He was so happy. He'd been making love, not just having sex. Next time, Cammy would make love to him. He'd be incoherent. He'd be—

She'd make love to him because she would be *in love with him.* The realization blindsided her. Gil talked on, completely unaware that Cammy was having A Moment. It was as though she'd put her life in storage and had gone on vacation for three years to Delusion Land. Gil had brought her home and made her turn on the lights and start retrieving the pieces of her life. And it looked as though he was going to be one of those pieces. He assumed he was. But Cammy needed to be sure. Being hopelessly infatuated for way too long made her judgment suspect.

Time to get dressed. This was going to be awkward. Undressing had been so much easier.

She sat up, wondering how to begin, when Gil snagged his shirt with his foot and shook it out before handing it to her. "In case somebody comes by before we find all your clothes."

Good idea.

He waited until she dragged the shirt over her head before opening the door. Standing by the car, he pulled on his shorts and just like that, he was decent, looking as if he'd been at the beach.

Men had it so easy.

He reached beneath the seat and came up with her shorts and underwear. "I was thinking," he said as he handed them to her.

Don't think, she thought.

"You could partner with me again. With Paul and me, because I wouldn't do that to him. Besides, he can draw and we can't. It's wild. You tell him something and he puts it on paper. He thinks as he's drawing. Give him a good idea and he'll make it great. With the two of us, we'll give him great ideas and the sky's the limit."

"Uh..." Had he noticed that she wasn't saying much? Had he noticed he was talking a lot?

"Cammy, we make creative magic. That doesn't happen very often." He grinned. "And obviously it transferred to the physical, too."

When she didn't respond, his grin faded.

Well, that wasn't fair to let him doubt it. "Gil, sex with you was scary good. It was—" she gestured because she couldn't find the words "—beyond anything that I ever dreamed sex could be."

"But?" he prompted.

"I feel as though I'm in an alternate universe. This time yesterday, I was sitting at my desk. And now I'm...I'm...." she looked down at herself. "Naked except for your shirt."

The grin was back. "Oh, I know."

She gave an unwilling laugh.

"But it's too fast for you," he said.

She nodded. "Not only that, but this isn't me. I would *never* have dreamed I'd do this. Or that I'd like it. I don't want you thinking this is me."

"Cammy, I know who you are."

Gil thoughtfully went searching for her bra in the front seat as she struggled into her underwear.

Yeah, but did Cammy know who she was?

Gil found the bra and her top, which had fallen to the ground. After shaking off bits of gravel and crushed shell, he gave her the clothes.

Their eyes met. She knew he saw the doubt in hers because he turned away so she could finish putting her clothes on.

Because she was being so quiet, he thought she was having regrets. Cammy searched her mind and found only a warning that if she didn't reassure him pronto, *then* she'd have regrets.

He stood in the open doorway with his back to her, arms crossed over his chest, probably mentally kicking himself.

Setting aside her bra and top, Cammy hooked a finger into the waistband of his shorts and tugged. "Hey."

"What?" He looked over his shoulder.

Cammy pulled his shirt over her head and plopped it next to her clothes. "I didn't get enough skin time with you. Come here."

The happiness and relief she saw on his face told her she'd made the right call. When he crawled back inside, she made him lay back and straddled him, running her hands over his chest and watching his eyes become glazed with desire.

I like this man she thought. *Really soon, I'm going to love this man.* Bending her head, she kissed his throat, along his jaw, beneath his ear, and the place where his neck met his shoulder.

Sighing, she laid her head on his shoulder, enjoying the way her skin felt against his. One of his hands rested in the small of her back, lightly caressing, making her aware of him without the white heat of passion consuming her. Just stoking the fire a little. "This is nice," she murmured.

She felt his breathing change and knew he was about to say something. "I meant what I said."

"About the three of us as a creative team?"

"Yes and when I said the L-word. I meant that."

"The L-word?" She smiled against his neck. "You mean love?"

"Yeah, but I thought it wouldn't sound so scary to you if I didn't say all of it."

"It's not scary. It's unexpected."

"I understand that. I do. But I wanted you to know sex with you wasn't just a casual thing. For me."

"I know." She kissed his jaw. "The past twenty-four

hours are a lot to process. You've had time. I've had a day." And right now, she didn't know what she felt or what she might feel. So she wasn't going to think about it. Yesterday's Cammy would pick apart every nuance of their…*encounter* might be the best word. Today's Cammy wasn't going to worry about it. Yet.

"Is there anything I can do to help the process along?"

"Yes," she said regretfully and sat up. "Turn on the air conditioning. It's really hot in here."

He smiled at her. "I can do that."

Later, after they were dressed, Gil grabbed a couple bottles of water from the supplies Cammy had brought and they sat in the car with the air conditioning running full blast.

Cammy tried calling Jonathan once more, but couldn't get through. "I suppose we'd better get back on the road. I hope the traffic has thinned out."

Gil fastened his seat belt. "Remember it wasn't as bad in the other direction."

"But we'll be going south."

"South?"

"Toward the coast? The beach house?"

He stared at her. "We're not still going to the beach house."

"Yes, we are. Why wouldn't we?"

He said nothing for several long moments. "Because you don't have to do that stuff anymore."

"That stuff is my job."

When more silent moments went by, Cammy added, "You can't expect me to abandon Jonathan just because you—"

"Had sex with you?"

Her jaw tightened. "I was going to say because you mentioned me working with you. Jonathan has to approve job changes anyway."

"Which he wouldn't."

"If I asked him—"

"Which you won't."

"Well, not if you act this way." He'd obviously decided what she was going to do before she had.

Gil gazed straight ahead. "Fine." He put the car in gear and drove out of the parking lot.

"WELL, WHAT DID YOU expect? That I'd profess my undying love for you?" It had been a silent and tedious, detour-filled drive to the beach house. When the house was finally in sight, Cammy couldn't stand it any longer. "You wouldn't have believed me if I had."

"Probably not."

"Certainly not. So what's with you?" He'd been so chatty earlier.

"I can't believe you still wanted to come down here. I thought you would have been jolted out of whatever trance Jonathan has put you in."

"So we're back to that?"

"Apparently, we never left." Gil drove over a line of seaweed and trash to get to the beach house.

It appeared to have survived the storm. Only one car was parked in the car port.

It wasn't Jonathan's.

As soon as Gil stopped, Cammy got out of the car and hurried to the bottom of the stairs as the door at the top slid open and a man came out.

"Mr. Dean!" It was Jonathan's client—the client who had called Cammy to say he was vacating the beach house. "Cammy Philips, Jonathan Black's assistant," she reminded him. "I thought you were leaving."

He came down the stairs. "I am leaving." He hefted a duffel over his shoulder. "We— I got caught by the weather. Uh," he gestured up toward the house. "There's no power. I— Was there supposed to be some sort of party here?"

Cammy threw an I-told-you-so look at Gil, who had walked up behind them. "I believe so."

"Only one other person made it and she left."

"Oh." And Cammy felt, rather than saw, Gil's I-told-you-so look at her.

"It was quite the storm," Mr. Dean continued. "We manually lowered the shutters and raised them this afternoon, so they'll need to be hooked back into the tracks."

"Thanks. I'll make a note of it," Cammy said. "If you want to go ahead and leave, we can close up here."

"That would be great." He smiled at her and nodded to Gil as he passed by.

Cammy didn't say anything as she climbed the stairs and went inside the house, but she heard Gil behind her.

It was cooler outside than it was inside the house even with the windows open.

"Now what?" Gil asked.

It was a valid question, but for some reason, it ticked her off. She whipped out her phone and hit Redial.

"Jonathan Black."

Actually hearing his voice after getting the mailbox message caught her off guard. "Jonathan, it's Cammy. Are you okay?"

"Ye-e-s-s. Why wouldn't I be okay?"

Out of the corner of her eye, she saw Gil lean against the sofa back and knew he could hear Jonathan through her phone.

"Because of the storm. Because your voice mailbox was full."

"Yeah." He sounded harried and she visualized him running a hand through his hair. Which might be ever so slightly thinning on the top. Which made her think of Gil's. Which was silky and soft and thick and tickled her thighs when he—

"I sent a private text to my whole address book by mistake and there was a little fallout, so I turned off the phone."

"About the party at the beach house last night." Her voice sounded calm even though the word *mistake* rang in her ears. Cammy was impressed with herself.

"There was no party." He gave a rueful laugh. "Or rather it was supposed to be a private party. I guess you saw the text."

"Yes. And got several messages about it when people couldn't reach you."

"Oh, hell. You don't suppose anyone actually drove down there? The weather was vile. I hope the house is still standing."

"It's fine," she snapped. "And only one woman accepted your bogus invitation. Heads-up—Adrian Dean was stuck here overnight—"

"Damn it! You told me he was leaving!" He was shouting in her ear.

Gil came off the back of the couch as though he was going to grab the cell phone away from her. Cammy held out her hand to stop him. This was her problem. Her boss. "He got caught here."

"Oh, that's just—wait. You said 'here.' You're at the beach house right now?"

"I told you so," Gil said.

She glared at him and turned away. "Yes."

"Cammy! Come on. You should have known that text was a mistake."

Because I would never invite you to one of my parties, he could have continued. But he didn't need to. She waited for the crushing devastation she would have felt just yesterday.

Nothing. Not even a little. If anything, she felt irritated with him and annoyed with herself. The past three years hadn't been a total waste; he'd taught her a lot. Maybe she'd convinced herself she loved him because it was safe, because she wasn't ready for the intensity of real love.

Her eyes sought Gil's. She was ready now.

"WHY WOULD I THINK it's a mistake? I usually organize your parties."

Gil listened as Cammy was drawn back into Jonathan's orbit. He'd actually thought they had something together, that she was over Jonathan.

In his mind, he remembered how she moaned and gasped his name. Gil. His name. She'd been with *him*. But he was losing her.

"Yeah, but..." Jonathan apparently thought better of coming right out and telling her he'd never invite her. Gil wished he would.

"Well, as long as you're down there," came Jonathan's voice through the phone, "take a look around and see if anything needs repair so we can arrange to get that done. While you're at it, would you straighten up the place? You know, towels, sheets, stray glasses. That kind of thing. I might make it down there tomorrow."

Great. Cammy would want to stay now.

"There's no power here."

"Oooh. No ice in the fridge. You better check and see if there's any food in there you need to throw out."

Gil was surprised Jonathan didn't ask her to restock.

"Okay," Cammy said. "Anything else?"

Gil rolled his eyes.

"I'll call if I think of anything. Otherwise, I'll see you Monday."

"Great." She looked straight at Gil. "We can discuss me moving back to the creative department then."

Gil thought his heart would stop.

"Cammy, what are you talking about?"

"Just that I'm ready for a job more challenging than providing maid service to the company beach house."

"Oh, hey, Cammy, I didn't mean—"

"Sure you did. We'll talk on Monday." And she not only ended the call, she powered off her phone.

She'd hung up on Jonathan. He couldn't believe it.

"You know," she said to Gil, "That's the same expression you had when I took off my bra outside the car."

He didn't doubt it for a minute. "You just told Jonathan that you wanted to move to the creative side."

"Hello? You asked me. Did you change your mind?"

"No. No!"

Cammy looked around the living room. "I can understand why you're surprised. There's nothing more annoying than a person who says I told you so. But I'm overlooking that." She reached over the sofa back and fluffed a couple of pillows. "What?" she asked him when he continued to stare at her. "I told you I need time to process. I've been processing." She headed for the kitchen.

Gil followed cautiously. She was way too calm.

There were a few dishes in the sink. Cammy ran some soapy water and handed Gil a towel. "Dry."

"Why are we doing this? I'm sure P&D has a service that comes in."

"They do. But not on a Saturday night after a major storm."

She quickly washed and rinsed a plate, holding it out for Gil. He wished he knew what she was thinking.

After drying the plate, he said, "It's late and I don't want to spend my Saturday night cleaning the company beach house."

She continued washing dishes. "We're not. We're going to be making love and skinny dipping in the ocean. I don't want this stuff in the way."

Gil nearly dropped the cup he was drying.

She laughed. "I told you I've been processing."

"You want to fill me in?"

Nodding, she said, "You were right, as you took such pleasure in telling me. I've spent long enough as Jonathan's starry-eyed assistant. I'm over it. Over him. I'm done."

Gil dried another plate and glass before he said anything. "So now that you can't have Jonathan, you'll settle for me? Is that it?"

She handed him a mug. "You're assuming quite a lot."

Gil slammed the mug on the counter and hauled Cammy to him, wet hands and all. He kissed her angrily and then hungrily. And she responded, opening her mouth beneath his and meeting his tongue with hers. He assumed nothing. She belonged with him.

Cammy pulled back. "Gil, I'm falling in love with you. Really fast."

His heart squeezed as he heard the tremble in her voice. "I do not want to be a revenge boyfriend or a rebound boyfriend."

"Can you just be a regular boyfriend?"

He'd take it—for now. "I will be a fantastic boyfriend—who doesn't share."

Grinning, Cammy backed away from him, pulling off her top and shimmying out of her shorts. "How about a boyfriend who skinny dips?"

He did love this woman. Gil yanked his shirt off. "I can do that."

Epilogue

JONATHAN HAD NEVER before enjoyed a late-Friday client meeting. The stupendously luscious Terry Simmons was bright, sometimes charmingly flustered, had a great idea for a job-sharing company, and Jonathan could swear her breasts were growing as the afternoon faded into evening.

Every time she moved or leaned over Ross's shoulder as he sketched an idea, Jonathan got a little buzz, a little zing. A glance around the room told him he wasn't the only one looking down her blouse. Not that anyone could see more than a shadowy cleft, but never had shadows hinted at so much.

Distracted by what those shadows hid, he didn't realize that the little buzzes were due to his cell phone vibrating in his pocket. When he did, he just sat back and enjoyed the sensation. Cheap thrills. So what?

Jonathan's strict policy was that no one took calls in front of a client, but his phone was going off like it was possessed.

Something big must be happening. He couldn't tell if anyone else in the room was getting message after message, which was both good and bad.

As the clouds rolled in, the room grew darker. Casually, Jonathan got up and walked behind Terry to the light console where he turned on the spots that illuminated the display board. Facing away from the room, he quickly flipped open his phone and scrolled through message after message, all from women, including his ex-girlfriends.

Not a good sign when the exes texted.

He read Jennifer's reply declining his beach-weekend invitation, which he wasn't entirely unhappy about. He read one other calling him a jerk, or words to that effect, and shoved the phone back into his pocket.

Turning around, he found several people watching him. Not everybody, but enough for him to know they'd seen him check his phone in clear violation of his own decree.

Covering, Jonathan stared out the window, obviously scanning the sky.

"Jonathan?" Ross and Terry were looking at him.

"Let's take a short break," he said. "I want to check on the weather."

"Good," Terry said. "I've got a seven forty-five flight and I'd like to know if it's still on time."

Now that he'd said he was going to, Jonathan quickly accessed the local weather on his phone. Heavy thunderstorms, flash-flood warnings, yeah, yeah. Wind shear advisory… hmmm. Not looking too good for Terry's flight.

So what was up with all the women calling and texting him?

After reading a half-dozen widely varying messages including one from a woman informing him that she was married and he was never to contact her again, Jonathan had an uneasy hunch he knew what had happened. His text to Jennifer had gone out to all the women he'd either dated or was thinking of dating.

This was going to cost him.

A sickening knot settled in his stomach. He'd asked them all to the beach house—no one would actually take him up on it, would they? Especially when it looked as though the weather was going to be so much worse than expected. And especially since he hadn't responded to any of them. No. No one would drive down there without verifying first. Besides, some of these women didn't even know where the beach house was.

Jonathan was still scrolling through the list and sending little "my bad" texts when the others began trickling back into the room.

"Let's try and finish up so we can all get home. It's going to be a messy weekend," Jonathan announced. "Terry, what else do you need from us?"

Twenty minutes later, the meeting was over, the room had emptied and Terry was talking on her cell in a low, worried voice. Sheets of rain poured down the windows.

"My flight is canceled," she explained when she closed her phone. "Nothing is leaving until conditions improve and apparently all the hotels near the airport are full. I need to get online and try to find a vacancy. Is it okay if I use this room or is there somewhere else I should go?"

Jonathan gazed sympathetically into her limpid, brown eyes and saw a hint of worry and a whole lot of stress. The canceled flight was just too perfect. Asking her to the beach house would have been presuming too much too early. But offering to shelter a storm refugee was his civic duty. "Terry, as you know, Peck and Davilla is a full-service media agency. We pride ourselves on meeting all our clients' needs. And you are a client in need. You're going to find that most decent hotels and motels will be booked solid. People who live near the coast always reserve rooms in case the power goes out or they have storm damage, and the airport will be dealing with stranded passengers for hours. I live in a downtown loft with a guest room I keep for circumstances just like this. You're welcome to stay there."

Terry had opened her laptop. "Thanks, but that's really

above and beyond what anyone would expect from your agency."

"Which is exactly why I'm offering. Peck and Davilla wants to exceed your expectations. In advertising, you never know what will happen or when an opportunity will come your way. Our agency prides itself on moving quickly and capitalizing on…call it serendipity."

She was tempted, he could see it, could see the anxiety change to hope.

She'd be relieved and grateful. Jonathan loved grateful women.

"There's plenty of space." He mentally inventoried the contents of his fridge and planned a dinner featuring his signature four-cheese macaroni dish. The recipe was easy and nobody made mac and cheese from scratch anymore. It was a stealth seducer masquerading as innocent comfort food. "You won't be the first client to stay there and you won't be the last."

"Plenty of space?" she repeated.

"It echoes." Not that they'd need plenty of space should the weekend go the way Jonathan intended.

She heaved a great sigh of relief. He watched the tension drain from her shoulders. Oh, yeah. A glass of wine and a meal of carbs and she'd be blissfully relaxed.

"Thank you *so* much. I'll call Warren and let him know. He and the kids are at a McDonald's down the street."

"Kids?"

Terry already held the cell phone to her ear. "Honey, we've got a place to stay." Then she saw Jonathan's expression and faltered. "It's still okay, isn't it?"

"I—uh…kids?" White carpet. Painted concrete floors. Metal and glass corners. Expensive electronics. Not kid friendly. Or husband friendly, either.

"Hang on, Warren." She looked up at Jonathan. "I have a three-year-old and a baby. Is that a problem?"

Jonathan's vision of the weekend underwent a radical change. "No, oh, no. We'll have to do a little childproofing, but it'll be fine. Please." He held out his hand for the phone. "Let me talk to your husband and we'll drive over and pick them up."

As Jonathan talked to Terry's husband, he heard shrieks and screaming in the background. Exactly how much alcohol did he have at the loft?

"I'm so grateful," Terry told him as they waited for the elevator. "I'm still nursing so Warren had to bring the baby and Nathan put up such a fuss when we dropped him off at my mom's that we had to bring him, too. The meeting went on longer than I expected and—" she gestured to her swollen chest "—I'm getting desperate."

Jonathan was getting desperate, too.

"I should warn you that Nathan is going through a screaming phase. The doctor says he's reacting to the new baby and wants attention. We're supposed to ignore him when he screams so we won't reinforce the behavior."

Did Jonathan have earplugs to go with that alcohol? Or maybe he could bash his head against the wall and knock himself out. "I think what everybody needs is my special macaroni and cheese. It's hard to scream when your mouth is full of macaroni and cheese."

"Nathan can scream through anything."

As the elevator doors opened Jonathan muttered, "I meant me."

Harlequin offers a romance for every mood!
See below for a sneak peek
from our paranormal romance line,
Silhouette® Nocturne™.
Enjoy a preview of REUNION by USA TODAY
bestselling author Lindsay McKenna.

Aella closed her eyes and sensed a distinct shift, like movement from the world around her to the unseen world.

She opened her eyes. And had a slight shock at the man standing ten feet away. He wasn't just any man. Her heart leaped and pounded. He reminded her of a fierce warrior from an ancient civilization. Incan? She wasn't sure but she felt his deep power and masculinity.

I'm Aella. Are you the guardian of this sacred site? she asked, hoping her telepathy was strong.

Fox's entire body soared with joy. Fox struggled to put his personal pleasure aside.

Greetings, Aella. I'm the assistant guardian to this sacred area. You may call me Fox. How can I be of service to you, Aella? he asked.

I'm searching for a green sphere. A legend says that the Emperor Pachacuti had seven emerald spheres created for the Emerald Key necklace. He had seven of his priestesses and priests travel the world to hide these spheres from evil forces. It is said that when all seven spheres are found, restrung and worn, that Light will return to the Earth. The fourth sphere is here, at your sacred site. Are you aware of it? Aella held her breath. She loved looking at him, especially his sensual mouth. The desire to kiss him came out of nowhere.

Fox was stunned by the request. *I know of the Emerald Key necklace because I served the emperor at the time it was created. However, I did not realize that one of the spheres is here.*

Aella felt sad. Why? Every time she looked at Fox, her heart felt as if it would tear out of her chest. *May I stay in touch with you as I work with this site?* she asked.

Of course. Fox wanted nothing more than to be here with her. To absorb her ephemeral beauty and hear her speak once more.

Aella's spirit lifted. What *was* this strange connection between them? Her curiosity was strong, but she had more pressing matters. In the next few days, Aella knew her life would change forever. How, she had no idea….

Look for REUNION
by USA TODAY *bestselling author*
Lindsay McKenna,
available April 2010,
only from Silhouette® Nocturne™.

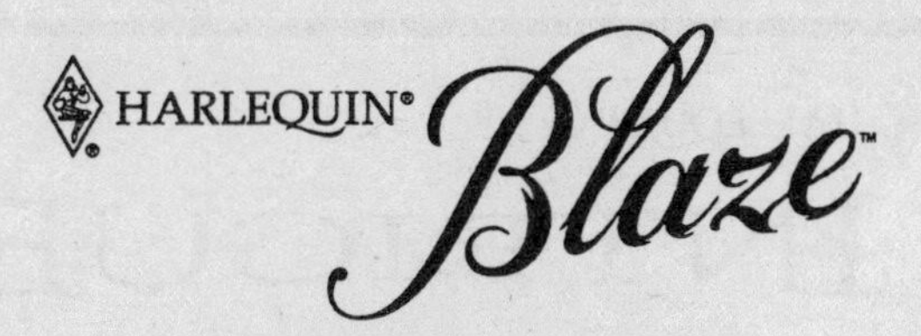

COMING NEXT MONTH

Available March 30, 2010

#531 JUST FOOLING AROUND
Encounters
Julie Kenner and Kathleen O'Reilly

#532 THE DRIFTER
Smooth Operators
Kate Hoffmann

#533 WHILE SHE WAS SLEEPING...
The Wrong Bed: Again and Again
Isabel Sharpe

#534 THE CAPTIVE
Blaze Historicals
Joanne Rock

#535 UNDER HIS SPELL
Forbidden Fantasies
Kathy Lyons

#536 DELICIOUSLY DANGEROUS
Undercover Lovers
Karen Anders

www.eHarlequin.com

HBCNMBPA0310